TERRA LUX

JESSAHME WREN

For information on other books by this author, visit Jessahme Wren online at
https://jessahmewren.com

Paperback ISBN 979-8-9921943-3-3

To Phoenix, Pearla, Sev, and Soren,
and to my faithful readers.

CHAPTER 1

The evening was crisp and cool. A beautiful Dobani sunset shone through the large glass windows, warming the storefront, painting the racks of clothes orange, red, and pink. The onset of the off-season had been good for business. The cool snap had sent everyone after coats and shawls, and Pearla had sold more of them this year than last. She closed the till, briefly calculating how many credits she'd made for the day of business.

It was the evening of the Festival of Light. Outside, the streets hummed with quiet excitement; vendors set up stalls, while festival goers lit lanterns and strung streamers along the streets to prepare for the yearly celebration.

Pearla stepped out from behind the counter, a hand on her round belly. Emma, her employee, came in from the sidewalk. She was rolling a rack of sale items, clothing better suited for warmer days Pearla was selling at a discounted price.

"Where do you want these, Pearla?" Emma stopped just inside the door, eyes roving over the shop.

Pearla gestured to the far wall. "Park them over there, Emma. By the dressing rooms. I may take some of them with me tonight."

Emma rolled the rack over to the dressing rooms and stepped to where Pearla was standing by a few boxes of goods. "I'm gonna help you load these. You don't need to be lifting so late in your pregnancy."

Pearla laughed. "They're not that heavy, Emma." She put her hands on her hips. "You sound just like Phoenix."

She smirked. "That's not a bad thing, then. We both just want the best for you."

Pearla shot her a wry smile. "And now you sound like Sev," she said, not missing a beat.

She activated the compact gravsled, and it floated over to where she stood. She began stacking the merchandise she would sell at her stall at the Festival of Light, folded shirts, slacks, a few hats, and dresses. True to her words, Emma helped, and with both working, they finished quickly.

"These are going to do great at the Festival," Emma said. She patted the nearest stack of shirts. "And I have a surprise."

Pearla considered Emma, wondering what the young woman was up to. "I'm going to work your shift at the Festival," Emma said. "I want you to enjoy this year with your family, not working the entire time."

Pearla smiled and clasped the woman in a fierce hug. "Thank you so much, Emma. This really means a lot. Sev and Phoenix love the Festival. It will be wonderful for us to all be together this year."

Emma withdrew, a big smile on her face. "Just think, next year you'll have a little one in tow. You won't be able to work much then, either."

She imagined her baby toddling through the Festival next year. Phoenix would fawn over them, for sure. Sev would want to carry them, though they'd be able to walk by then. She would buy them sweets, as many as they wanted.

"You better get going, Pearla." Emma handed Pearla her jacket and ushered her out the door. "You're meeting them at the fountain, right?"

Pearla nodded. She held the young woman's hand. "I can't thank you enough for doing this, Emma. For giving me this. You've earned yourself a day off. Just say the word."

She gave her a grateful smile. Pearla shrugged into her jacket and stepped out into the waning light.

The sidewalk was bustling with people from all over. Banners hung from the lampposts, their colorful tails unfurling in the breeze. People had already lit the lamps, and the flames danced within their thin globes. Pearla elbowed her way through the crowd, eyes up ahead. The fountain was in the plaza, the very center of the Festival activities. There would be vendor stalls everywhere, including hers.

Someone stopped her, offering her a flower. "For the baby," they said, and Pearla accepted it with a smile. Others did the same, often stopping to give her little tokens of appreciation or just to offer their congratulations.

Through the crowd, she spotted the fountain. The sun had set, and tiny colored spotlights lit the water as it cascaded down the stone structure. Phoenix was there, and beside him, Sev. They were casting flower petals over the water. She approached them, and Phoenix leaned in for a kiss.

"There she is," he whispered, pressing a kiss to her cheek. "Sev and I were almost out of petals."

Pearla peered into the fountain's pool; lit candles floated, buoyed by the water's gentle current, along with flower petals from other revelers. She handed Sev the flower she held. "Not out yet," she said, and Sev gave her a delighted smile.

"Thanks, Pearla." Sev stripped the flower's petals and held them out to her. "You want to toss some?"

Pearla shook her head, one hand on her belly. "I'm fine, Sev. I've got nothing to wish for." She considered Phoenix, smiling. "I've got all I could ever want between the two of you. And this little one, of course."

It seemed to please Sev. She gave half the petals to her father, who closed his eyes and hummed dramatically. Pearla laughed. He tossed his handful into the water and turned to her, a big smile on his face.

She turned to him. "What did you wish for, my love? Or can you say?" Growing up on Dobani, she'd taken for granted the yearly festival, writing it off as something for off-worlders and tourists. But Phoenix and Sev loved the tradition.

"A healthy baby, of course." He pressed a kiss to her forehead.

"Hmm, no preference as to the gender, then?"

Sev laughed. "He wished for a girl," she said, her eyes twinkling in the lamplight. "Don't let him fool you, Pearla."

Phoenix feigned shock. "I wouldn't waste a Festival wish on such. Besides, there's no need. I *know* she's a girl already," he said with a grin. "Just a feeling."

Pearla grabbed his hand. All out of petals now, they made their way through the crowd, Sev taking the lead and Phoenix and Pearla walking together just behind. Sev pointed to a vendor selling fried bread, and they all stopped.

"What do you want in yours, Daddy? I'll buy."

Phoenix raised his eyebrows. "Treating your old man? I should be honored. I'll take peppers in mine, dear heart. What are you having?"

Sev grinned. "The very same. Pearla?"

She waved her off politely. "Plain for me, Sev."

Phoenix reached out and lay his hand on her belly. "Little Lori must be hungry. No filling this time?"

Pearla shook her head, covering her hand with his. "None for me. But I will take a fresh one."

Sev gave the vendor her card, and she soon had three steaming flats of bread wrapped in paper. She gave Pearla hers, the last one made and the freshest. "Your wish is my command," Sev said with a flourish.

Pearla took a bite, humming at the taste. Phoenix grinned around a mouthful of bread. The lightning bugs were out, twinkling intermittently in the crisp night air. They strolled under the lamplights, the colorful banners. Sev stopped at a few more vendors, but didn't make any purchases. Up ahead, there was music coming from the plaza center.

Sev's eyes grew bright. "The band! Come, Daddy, Pearla…let's dance!"

Phoenix took his daughter's hand, smiling. Pearla followed close behind. Sev moved onto the cobblestones and grabbed Pearla's hand with her other one. The three of them formed a perfect circle.

Sev stepped left for a few beats, then Phoenix led them right. The music was jaunty and whimsical. They took turns leading the dance, giggling when one of them stumbled.

They stopped on the next song, out of breath. "I better sit down," Pearla said, a big smile on her face. Sev came back with some berry juice, and she drank it heartily.

They walked home under a starlit sky. Sev detoured them by the beach. The tide was coming in, and the moon was full and bright. They slipped off their shoes to wade ankle-deep in the foam. Pearla's skirt was skimming the water, but she didn't mind.

"We're going to have to keep more responsible hours when the baby comes," Pearla mused.

Phoenix scoffed. "Nonsense. Little Lorien will be in on the hijinks, of course. Truly one of us."

Sev laughed. "Don't worry, Pearla. I won't let her get too far out of sight. She'll be right alongside us. Right Daddy?"

Phoenix hummed. In the moonlight, the white patch in his hair practically glowed. "More than, Sev. My two jewels."

Pearla held Phoenix's hand. She wondered briefly if the baby could hear their voices or the way the waves rushed ashore. She hoped so.

Up ahead, Sev gathered shells in one hand and held her shoes in the other. Phoenix gazed at Pearla, his face awash in the blue-grey light from the moon. "I love you," he whispered.

She moved closer to him, the cool water chilling her momentarily. "And I, you," she said.

CHAPTER 2

It was evening, and waning light flooded the kitchen. Phoenix held the pan, tipping it from side to side before expertly flipping it. The eggs turned in the air and landed with a satisfying smack, sunny side down. "Just a flick of the wrist, little mouse," he said with a glint in his eye. "Remember when I taught you?"

Sev nodded. Phoenix noticed she was quieter than usual. "When will it be ready, Daddy? I'm starving."

Phoenix frowned, setting the spatula aside. "You didn't eat lunch at school, mouse?"

Sev made a face. "I did. But the portions were smaller than usual. It was so strange."

Phoenix hummed. "Maybe they just seemed small because you were so hungry."

She shook her head. "They didn't give us enough, Daddy. Some students complained."

He turned off the burner and plated the eggs. Flatcakes came next; Phoenix mixed up extra batter just for his Sev.

He poured the first one to sizzle on the griddle, then turned, wiping his hands on the dish towel he had tucked into the waistband of his pants. "I'll talk to the school, sweet mouse," he vowed, pressing his lips to her hair. "Can't have my girl hungry at school now."

She slumped in her chair. "Thanks, Daddy. I'm sure there's an explanation. I think I'll take my lunch for a few days, though, just in case."

Phoenix nodded. "A fine idea. I'll make it myself. What do you want tomorrow? Leftover flatcakes?"

Pearla came into the kitchen, a sweater stretched over her ample belly. "You're assuming there'll be leftovers," she teased, laughing.

Sev smirked at her. "Not with you eating for two, there won't be." She held out her plate for her father to fork some flatcakes onto it alongside the eggs, and he complied.

He handed Pearla her plate as well, and Pearla sat at the table beside Sev. "What's that you were saying about school, Sev?"

Sev swallowed a mouthful of flatcakes before answering. "They didn't feed us enough lunch today."

Pearla gave him a curious look. "That's weird, because my lunch at the diner today was smaller, too. The portions weren't the same. I thought it was my imagination at first."

Phoenix settled at the table with a plate of his own. He shrugged. "I'm sure it's a quirk. It'll work itself out." He stabbed at his flatcakes and raised the fork to his mouth. "Until then, let's just be vigilant."

Sev nodded. She was halfway through her meal and was sipping the last of her juice. She dabbed at her lips with a napkin. "I think I'll go down to the beach, Daddy. Watch the sunset."

It soothed him. His girl was happiest by the water; had been since she was a child. "Have fun. Don't stay out too late and catch cold."

She went over to her father and put her arm around him, kissing his cheek. "I won't," she whispered. "Dinner was delicious."

Sev paused by Pearla's chair, placing her hand on her shoulder and giving it a little squeeze. "Wanna come float? I bet the baby would like it."

Pearla shook her head. "The water is a little cool this time of year for me, Sev. But thank you. I'm going to turn in early."

Phoenix cleared the table. He collected the scraps and was going to put them down the disposal, and Pearla caught his hand. "Don't throw away any food, hon. I've got a bad feeling."

Phoenix nodded. Neither of them said anything more. Pearla insisted on helping him load the dishwasher, and they retired to the couch.

Pearla reclined and put her feet in Phoenix's lap. He took the hint and began massaging them. "What did you mean before, love? When you said you had a bad feeling?"

She considered. "I just think we need to be conservative, is all. It's just a feeling. Nothing may be wrong, but it doesn't hurt to be safe."

Phoenix considered. "Of course," he finally said. But he couldn't stop thinking.

◆ ◆ ◆

The next day, Pearla went to work. Sev was at school; she'd taken her lunch like she said she would. Phoenix had even packed Pearla something to snack on at the store so she wouldn't have to go to the diner. He'd all but forgotten about the smaller portions they both reported; surely there was a simple explanation.

Phoenix packed his books and holopad and headed off to class. He would start his clinicals soon…teaching actual students at a proper school. It made him slightly nervous with anticipation. He was down the steppingstone path and almost to the transport when he spied his neighbor.

Phoenix raised his hand in greeting, and the neighbor waved. "Hiya Phoenix. You hear about the seed shortage at the grain depot? If you're going to plant a garden, you better stock up now. They're nearly out."

Phoenix hitched his pack higher on his shoulders. "Why would there be a shortage on seed? Growing season starting early?"

The neighbor shrugged. "I dunno. But I know that girl of yours likes to garden. Better get her stocked up before they sell out."

Phoenix nodded, something twisting behind his polite smile. The news bothered him, but he couldn't put his finger on why. After class, he would run by the farmer's supply and pick up some seed for Sev.

He turned the radio on and pulled out of the driveway. Soft music filled the cab, tempering his anxiety a little. By the time he got to the university, the strange encounter with his neighbor was all but forgotten.

Phoenix made his way into the lecture hall. His steps inside echoed in the empty room; he was the first one there. That was unusual, but not unheard of. Usually, there were a few straggling students left over from the previous class. He would chat, sometimes study with them. But now, he found himself alone. He fired up his holopad and read over his notes. They had a quiz today; he'd been up late studying.

He waited for a while. The passing of time grew ominous. A ticking chrono on the wall marked each passing minute, loud in the quiet. Alarm straightened his shoulders, causing him to be sensitive to every sound in the suddenly too large room. *Was class canceled?* He'd rarely had a class to cancel, and when it did, his professor always notified them. With nowhere else to go, he sat there a few minutes longer, growing more uncomfortable by the minute. Finally, someone walked into the empty lecture hall.

It was his professor. He had a stricken expression on his face. "Oh, Phoenix. I'm sorry. I figured you knew by now."

Phoenix straightened, leaning forward slightly. "Knew what?"

The professor pressed his lips together. "The university is closing for a while. It's um…a funding issue. Notifications went out this morning."

Something twisted in Phoenix's gut. *Funding?* The university was a public institution supported by the Dobani government. Funding had never been an issue. Phoenix's mouth grew dry. "What about the clinicals? I'm due to be assigned a school next week."

The professor lowered his eyes. He opened his desk drawer and withdrew a holopad. When he raised his head, he had a regretful expression on his face. "They're canceled, too." He frowned. "I'm sorry, Phoenix. I know you were looking forward to it."

He tucked the holopad under his arm and left the lecture hall before Phoenix could ask him anything else.

Phoenix checked his messages. Sure enough, there was one from the university announcing its hasty closure, sent just an hour ago. The message never mentioned a reopening time.

Feeling somewhat defeated and a bit bereft, he gathered his belongings and made his way back to the transport. Phoenix felt as if a heavy weight was bearing down on him. Something felt very wrong. There was something he didn't know—something important. Something life-altering.

He got behind the wheel of the transport and headed to town. Maybe the people at the seed store would know what was going on. The faster he found out, the better.

CHAPTER 3

More people were in town than usual. Transports lined the streets. People carried heavy packages or pulled gravsleds stacked high with goods. Phoenix hadn't seen activity like this since the last storm, when everyone had stocked their cupboards in case of a power outage.

He parked his transport and stepped out onto the busy street of the otherwise peaceful suburb of Dobani Proper. A woman rushed by him, losing goods off the top of her armload of wares as she went.

Phoenix picked up her loaf of bread with his prosthetic arm, turned and called out to her. The woman was in such a rush, she never looked back.

After his initial shock had worn off, Phoenix noticed the stores were overflowing. Shop doors stood open on either side of the street. Horns blared…people in transports cut others off in their haste to get in and out, shaking their fists in the air. The streets resonated with murmured voices, hushed exclamations. For as visually scrambled as it was, the streets were eerily quiet except for the noise of transports and aggressive driving.

On the corner, a line of military vehicles loomed, matte black and still. Soldiers stood nearby, watching the crowd with impassive eyes.

Strange, Phoenix thought. He'd never seen military on the streets before. The military had a historically low presence on Dobani. It was one thing he liked about it.

Up ahead, a soldier was walking toward him, the grit of his boots loud on the pavement. He motioned to the loaf of bread in Phoenix's hand.

"You need to get your supplies and move along. You're not safe here just standing in the street."

Since when? Phoenix wanted to ask, but he squelched the urge. He nodded and moved to walk past the soldier into a nearby store. He'd almost made it when the soldier gripped his mechanical arm.

"Be home before dark," he said. It wasn't a suggestion. A cold unease settled in Phoenix's gut. His eyes flitted to the man's weapon. He'd never seen a soldier carry that type of rifle. Not on Dobani. Something was deeply wrong.

He finally broke away and shouldered his way inside. The memory of the soldier's grip lingered—phantom fingers threatening, squeezing his prosthetic like it was flesh. Bags of flour were on the floor; cereal boxes had toppled from the shelf. The air smelled dusty, and spilled goods lay everywhere. People milled about like ants, half-crazed by some unnamed stressor. One man nearly bumped into him, muttering a string of curses.

Phoenix sidled out of the way, stooping to pick up an item and place it back on the shelf, and the store owner waved him off. The man appeared frazzled.

"Don't bother," he said, his voice shaky. "It's been a wreck since noon." He handed him a basket. "Get what you need, Phoenix." His eyes darted around the store, obviously nervous. "Whatever's left, that is." He leaned in, nearly whispering. "The soldiers won't let you linger long."

The man moved to walk away, back to the register, but Phoenix stopped him. "What's going on?" Phoenix asked him, his voice low and urgent. The man shook his head. "Come back just before curfew," he whispered. "I'll tell you then."

He shook him off and returned to his post at the register. He was checking out customers before Phoenix had time to ask him. Instead, two words screamed inside his head. *What curfew?*

Then, the pieces all fell together. *Be home before dark*, the soldier had said. There must be a curfew in place for Dobani citizens. That explained the rush. The mad dash to get supplies.

Phoenix swallowed, his hand growing tighter on the basket. These people were scared.

◆ ◆ ◆

Phoenix went down the aisles. He was more concerned with watching people than with shopping for goods. Everyone he met seemed hurried and near panicked. Phoenix filled his basket, but what he was really looking for was answers. Unfortunately, no one seemed inclined to talk.

When he made it to the farmer's supply, people had scattered seed and soil everywhere. Phoenix wondered again what the soldiers were here for, if not to prevent behavior like this. But they merely watched, an unavoidable presence…silent sentries with a menacing air and rifles slung over their shoulders.

Phoenix bought Sev the only seed they had left. Following his instincts, he also purchased glow rods and batteries. There were soldiers there too, standing at the end of the aisles. People flitted around them, unnerved by their presence.

Walking back to the transport, he tried to call Sev. The connection was tenuous, but he finally got through.

She must've seen his knit brows, the stress written on his face. "Daddy? What's going on?"

He settled inside the transport, a deep frown on his face. He could see Sev's face in hologram. She was in the library at school, working at her job. Life used to be so simple for them until suddenly it wasn't.

"I don't know, mouse. But something's up. I don't want to alarm you now, but it's important that you listen to me."

Sev shook her head. Her eyes were wide; there was a sense of alertness and urgency there that he wasn't used to seeing. He felt a twinge of protectiveness in his chest. "No, Dad. I already know. Things feel strange. The school is letting out after lunch. I'll be home soon."

He saw her look at him, observing what she could see of his background. "Are you in town?" she asked. "Why aren't you at the university?"

There was a regrettable quirk to his mouth. "Closed until further notice." His brow creased, and there was a note of sadness tinging his face. "They canceled my clinicals."

Sev frowned. "Oh Daddy. I'm so sorry." She glanced at him with questioning eyes. "They didn't say why?"

Phoenix hummed. "No. Same as you. Just a closure or a cancelation. No other explanation." He pivoted his head to the right, then left, making sure no one was listening. He leaned in close to the holopad where it sat balanced on the steering wheel of his transport. "I don't know how to explain it, Sev. But I feel like we need to be careful. Don't speak to anyone. Don't be out alone." He pursed his lips. "Do you know about the curfew?"

She had a perplexed look on her face. "My curfew?"

He shook his head. "No, love. There's a curfew for all Dobani, now. No one out after dark. Have you heard from Pearla?"

"No," Sev said, alarmed. "You think she's ok?"

He nodded. "I'm sure she's fine, little mouse. I'll go pick her up at the store. And Sev?"

She met her father's gaze, hers soft and a little fearful in the flickering hologram. "Yes, Daddy?"

His eyes roved over the image of her face, his mouth tense. "Watch out for the soldiers. Have one of your friends follow you. Come straight home, no questions."

Sev said nothing for a moment. She had pulled her lip between her teeth and was worrying it, a nervous habit. "Are we going to be ok, Daddy? I'm scared."

He tutted. "We're more than fine, Sev. Just get home soon and get home safe. That's all that matters to me now. Once you are home, we'll only venture out in groups."

Sev gave him a tentative smile. "I love you, Dad."

It eased him some. "I love you too, Sev."

The holopad winked out, and he laid it on the seat beside him. He wouldn't call Pearla. It was probably best just to show up. He didn't want to alarm her with the baby.

Phoenix took one last look at the chaos of the town and pointed the transport toward Dobani Proper.

CHAPTER 4

Sev put away her holopad. She could tell her father was worried; his warnings were not just the product of his overprotectiveness. Sev knew in her gut that something was wrong.

She sat in the lecture hall as the last class was nearing completion. The teacher could barely make eye contact with them. There was a palpable apprehension in the room. Instead of students laughing and interacting, as usual, there was an uncomfortable silence.

Tentatively, one student raised his hand. "Please tell us what's going on, Ms. Sharp. Why is school letting out early?"

The teacher sighed. "I know what you know, Jessup. All we can do is continue class like usual until we hear differently." She placed her holopad on her desk and scanned the room. "Questions about today's lesson?"

There were none, and though Sev had other questions, she knew Ms. Sharp wouldn't answer them.

The class finally dismissed. Normally they would linger on the grounds, or group together for a trip to the stim cafe. Students often walked together, enjoying the balmy Dobani weather or heading out to the beach.

Word had quickly spread that something was afoot; however, and that a curfew was in place. Students were climbing into their transports or taking the chute straight home. There would be no after-school activities today.

Sev searched for her friend in the crowd. She'd asked her to follow her home, like her father had told her, but she was nowhere to be found. Then her holopad dinged.

She read the notification. It was her friend, Ana.

I'm sorry Sev. My parents want me home right away.

Sev closed the message and sighed. She'd have to go alone, then.

She climbed into her transport and pulled out into the traffic flow. Sev turned on the radio, hoping for news of what was really going on, but all she found was music.

With a frustrated huff, she flipped the radio off. She let the low hum of the repulsor engine ease her dread. Phoenix had bought her a transport, true to his word, shortly after they returned from Ocarro.

Sev peeled away from the main highway and pointed the transport toward home. Her mind was racing with uncertainty, trying to parse the meaning of what had transpired in such a short time. The school offered no answers, and her teachers seemed just as uncertain and fearful as she was. Sev's friends had wild theories, but none of them seemed plausible.

Suddenly, the transport stuttered, lurched forward, and began billowing blue smoke. Sev navigated to the side of the road just before it stopped completely.

She sat for a moment, processing. The acrid smoke from beneath the hood told her it was electrical. The lights on her console were blinking red, confirming her suspicion. It was the last thing she needed to deal with, especially now.

Briefly, Sev thought of calling her father, but if he had gone to get Pearla in Dobani Proper, he would have been too far away to get to her before curfew. She'd have to deal with this herself, she realized. With a new sense of resolve, she grabbed her toolkit from the back and stepped out of the transport.

The blue smoke had all but dissipated, but the smell of scorched wiring still burned her nose. The highway she was on was not well-traveled; in fact, she had seen no one since pulling to the side of the road.

Not that she would trust just anyone to help, anyway. Especially not now, with all the strange occurrences. Her father's warning that they should exercise caution in trusting anyone echoed in her mind.

Sev lifted the hatch on the transport and surveyed the inner workings there. Most of her experience working on engines had come from Del, and later, from shadowing Uncle Dak in the junkyard. Del was always renting secondhand transports that needed work, rattletrap things held together with spit and prayers.

She held the spanner in her hand and retracted the wiring. Sparks sizzled, and fresh wisps of smoke curled upward. Sev surveyed what lay below the hatch. One circuit had completely blown, and she'd have to replace it. Fishing around in her toolkit, she found the soldering iron and clamps. It would take time to repair the circuit. It was time she didn't have.

Sev took a breath. The curfew was in the back of her mind, but it didn't matter. Being stranded on a remote highway did not allow you to be picky. Any help was miles away. She had to fix the transport, regardless of the time limit.

With a determined set of her mouth, she got to work.

◆ ◆ ◆

It took longer than expected. Her hands cramped, and her head ached from the pungent ozone of the soldering iron. When Sev closed the hatch on the transport, it was nearly sunset.

She hurriedly climbed behind the wheel and activated the control panel. She started the engine sequence and held her breath. After a few terrifying moments, the repulsors hummed, and the transport lifted off the ground.

Sev exhaled shakily. She would get home well after dark now. There was no avoiding it. Without another thought, she pointed the transport down the road and tried to make up for lost time.

After a few minutes of traveling, Sev saw lights up ahead. There were vehicles parked on either side of the road…military transports. There was a large metal gate stretching across the highway.

Oh, Drek, she thought with trepidation. This would delay her even more. What her father had said about being careful around soldiers gave her pause.

She rolled to a stop, trying to keep her breathing steady. The gate loomed ahead like a judgment. Her ID was just a few months old; she was a certified transport driver now. She lowered the viewpane as the soldier approached her. He had a sizeable weapon looped over his shoulder.

"Identification please."

Sev tried not to betray her nerves when she pulled out her ID, though her hands shook lightly. She examined the soldier's face. He wore a mask over his nose and mouth so that all she could see were his eyes. There was a rigid set to his upper body.

He took her identification and checked it. After a few moments, he handed it back to her.

"Step out of the transport, please."

Her pulse quickened. Her hands gripped the wheel, the knuckles white. She thought wildly of crashing through the gate and speeding toward home, but it was just an intrusive thought. She knew that would land her imprisoned, or worse.

"Why?"

She'd asked before she could stop herself. It seemed to anger him, she noticed, the way his shoulders tensed. He tightened his grip on the weapon, and for the first time Sev noticed how large his hands were. The soldier leaned against the frame of the open viewpane, filling up the space. "I won't ask again."

Sev swallowed. She opened the door of the transport and slowly stepped out. She felt small, even though Sev was tall for her age. The soldier gave her a withering glance and shifted on his feet.

"Out after curfew?"

She met his eyes despite her nerves. "I had transport trouble. Had to repair it. I was on the side of the road awhile."

He huffed. "You repaired it?"

Sev lifted her head slightly. "Yes, of course I did."

The soldier said nothing. He inspected her transport with a little glow rod, checking out the backseat, the toolkit there. Another soldier approached him then, motioning with his hand.

"What's the holdup, here? You letting her go, or not?"

The soldier examining the transport regarded the other man, then glanced back at Sev. Something unnamed flashed in his eyes, but disappeared just as quickly. "Yeah," he finally said, and Sev released a breath she didn't realize she was holding.

Sev got back into the transport, strapping in with trembling hands. She worked to regulate her breathing while they opened the gate. To her right, a girl not much older than her was being restrained against a military vehicle. As the gate slid open, Sev saw another soldier stuff her into the back of one of their trucks.

It shook her. The soldier who had questioned her waved her through, his ice-laden eyes still haunting her as she drove away.

◆ ◆ ◆

When Sev pulled into her yard, it was already dark. A light was on in the kitchen, and she could see Pearla sitting at the table.

Sev opened the door. Her father was pacing in the living room, and when he saw her, his face completely transformed, the relief there palpable.

"Oh Sev. Sweetheart. I was so worried." He pulled her into a tight hug, and Sev relaxed into it. Just as quickly, he released her. "Why didn't you call?"

Her eyes roved over her father's face. Behind him, she could see Pearla coming out of the kitchen, holding a cup of tea. She appeared as relieved as Phoenix did.

"I had circuit trouble on the new transport, Daddy. You were too far away to get to me. I fixed it myself."

Phoenix pressed his lips to his daughter's forehead. "Always call me, little mouse. No matter where I am."

She nodded. Pearla laid a hand on her shoulder. "We were both so worried about you, Sev."

"I'm sorry," Sev said. "I didn't mean to be late, honest. This curfew business is so strange."

The tension was back in Phoenix's face. He eyed Pearla, then Sev, his brow pinched. "Let's sit down, mouse. We need to talk."

They settled in the living room, on the couch and in the chair there. Being home was a relief, but there were bigger things at play now—more to worry about than just what they could control.

"I don't have a clear picture of what's going on yet," Phoenix began. "But the increased military presence here on Dobani, plus the curfew, can't mean anything good."

Sev hummed. "I ran up on a checkpoint tonight."

Her father made a face. His hands clenched in his lap; she could see the tension in his body, the slight trace of anger. Still, he said nothing.

"I handled it, but I got a bad feeling from the soldier. Like he wasn't trying to protect me. Like he was just looking for an excuse. To do what, I'm not sure."

Phoenix mumbled something, and Pearla put a hand to her mouth. "I'm so thankful you made it past the checkpoint, hon," she said. "Did they say why they stopped you?"

Sev shook her head. "I made it through, but I saw them take someone else into custody. I don't know why."

Her father cursed. "From now on, we leave the house together. Food and supplies are scarce already; I don't know if that's going to get better. We watch what we consume. We save our credits. I suspect, if things get worse, we'll be bartering rather than buyin'."

Sev felt tears sting her eyes, but she willed them away. Pearla reached for Phoenix's hand, and he took it in his.

"We're going to get through this together," he said. "I don't want you worrying, little mouse. We're going to live our lives like normal until we can't anymore. And hopefully that day never comes."

She nodded. It was a plan, but things still felt bleak.

CHAPTER 5

Pearla got out of bed and reached for her robe. The morning was chilly. They were conserving power, had decided last night. If the Dobani infrastructure was failing, the power grid wouldn't be far behind.

It still felt like a dream. Dobani—her home. Now, their home. The life they'd made together. It was all at risk.

Pearla found her way into the kitchen, foregoing the lights. She'd use enough power to make the stim brew, then breakfast, but the rest they could do without.

She started the pot, listening to it chug and churn puffs of steam into the cool kitchen. Pearla closed her eyes. Things had happened so fast. It seemed like just yesterday they were at the festival, no worries to speak of.

Her holopad pinged, and she silenced it immediately. Phoenix and Sev were still asleep, and she was loath to disturb them. Phoenix, especially, had enough to worry about. She didn't want to shorten his sleep over a noisy holopad.

She read the notification. It was a call from Emma.

Pearla answered, stepping away from the stim brew and settling by the window. "Hi Emma. Is there anything wrong?"

Emma seemed stricken. Her image shook slightly where she held the holopad. Pearla could tell she was in the store, but the lights were off.

"Pearla, there's a line of people outside. They're all clamoring to get in. Some of them are quite insistent. Angry, even." Her eyes darted toward the door, the nervousness on her face obvious. "I need you," she whispered. "I wouldn't ask if it wasn't necessary. But I'm scared, Pearla. I've never seen this before."

Pearla nodded. "No, Emma, it's fine. I'll be there soon, Ok? Don't open the door." She almost told her to call the Enforcers, but she guessed the military was in charge now. The thought sent a chill down her spine. "Stay calm, Emma. Leave the lights off 'till I get there."

She ended the call and placed the holopad on the table. The stim brew was ready, but she no longer wanted it. As soon as she'd processed the distressing call, she disappeared into the bedroom to get dressed.

◆ ◆ ◆

She left a note. She knew Phoenix would be cross with her for going by herself, but this was an emergency. Emma needed her. She would handle the aftermath later.

Pearla eased the transport into downtown Dobani Proper, and she could see the crowd of people as soon as she rounded the curve.

It was more like a mob. The posture of the people waiting outside, their fists raised, made her stomach lurch. Mothers had their children with them, waiting in the frigid morning. Others pushed against the large glass windows of her store, trying to get in…trying to see inside. Pearla pulled around back and entered through the service entrance.

She found Emma crouching behind the counter, the lights still off. Pearla set down her belongings and went to her, placing a hand on her trembling back. "Emma, honey. I got here as quickly as I could."

Emma gazed up at her. She'd been crying.

The morning light was gleaming through the large front glass, over the heads of the people outside. Those up front could plainly see Pearla, and they began beating on the viewpanes.

What if they break in? Pearla thought fearfully, but she tamped it down. She gave Emma a hand and helped her up. The people outside started shouting, their voices a combined roar that drowned out the usual hustle and bustle of Dobani Proper.

In fact, aside from the people outside, the streets were quiet. No traffic.

"What do we do?" Emma asked her. Her eyes were wide with fear, her mouth turned down in uncertainty.

Pearla patted her shoulder. "We do what we can. We let them in…see what they want. If things get rough, we hide in the back room, and I'll call Phoenix."

Just then, a large military vehicle pulled up to the front of the building. People scattered, screaming in panic. Three soldiers got out and stalked toward the door. One bashed in the glass with the butt of his rifle.

It startled Pearla, and she placed a protective hand over her belly. She was still standing behind the counter, speechless, when the soldiers made their way inside, boots crunching on the newly broken glass.

"Are you the owner here?" the man asked in a gruff, clipped voice.

She straightened, meeting the soldier's hard glare. "I am," Pearla said.

He nodded. He wore a face covering, but his hard, steely eyes shone above the fabric. "Outfit my men. Then let the people outside have the rest."

Pearla gave him a shaky nod, and Emma stepped up to help. The soldiers started grabbing coats and gloves, boots, and other items. Pearla brought them to the register, and the soldier grabbed her arm. "Don't think you understand," he said, his voice cold. "These belong to us now."

She stiffened. This store was *hers*. She'd built this place from nothing.

Pearla lifted her head, locking eyes with the soldier. "My inventory does not belong to the government," she told him icily.

The soldier huffed a harsh, mirthless laugh. "It does now," he said.

He took the items from her and gave the other soldiers a signal as he was leaving. One kicked over a rack of shoes. The other hit the remaining window with his baton, shattering it on his way out.

With a crush of bodies, the people flooded inside. The soldiers didn't leave. Instead, they loaded their wares into the military transport and took up post outside the shattered doorway. The crowd grew quiet. Fear replaced their urgency. Pearla felt it, too.

Dust swirled in the air, stirred by the chaos. Shouts echoed off the glass-strewn floor, mingling with the sharp smell of sweat and fear. Pearla gripped the counter, steadying herself as her store—her dream—dismantled around her.

A woman stepped through the shattered door. She had a little girl with her, holding her hand. The woman had been crying. She approached Pearla, gripping the child's hand tightly.

"There's looting everywhere," she whispered. "Our cards are void…credits commandeered by the military." She looked down. When she lifted her head, fresh tears filled her eyes. "We have nothing. I'm so sorry."

Pearla reached out and placed a hand on the woman's shoulder. Nausea roiled in her stomach, laced with just a little fear. "Don't worry," Pearla said. "We'll get through this together, hmm? Take what you need." She gave her shoulder a little squeeze. "It's ok."

The woman gave her a watery smile, then abruptly hugged her. "They're making us fight," she whispered in her ear. "You and your baby…get out of here while you can. It's not safe."

She let her go, leaving Pearla speechless and shaken. More people filed inside with instructions from the soldiers to take what they wanted, a gift from the Dobani government. But Pearla didn't believe Dobani would turn against its own people like that. That wasn't in sync with the planet she knew and loved.

Pearla heard one soldier say they would need the warm clothing where they were going, and she wondered briefly what that meant.

The looting went on for hours. Pearla helped people steal from her store, trying to keep things from spiraling out of control; it was heartbreaking watching these people systematically strip her of all her hard work…of her livelihood.

By lunchtime, Pearla was shaky and exhausted. The soldiers had gone, satisfied that people had what they needed. Pearla and Emma picked through the ravages of her store, their faces blank.

Racks stood stripped and askew. Glass littered the floor, and the scant few clothes that were left lay trampled underfoot.

Pearla gave Emma the items left in her size, and she gathered some things for Phoenix and Sev. She made her way out into the midday sun with what little she'd rescued and walked down the sidewalk to the transport.

She could feel the tears welling in her eyes, but she willed them away. Pearla resolved not to cry…not now. Not when others were suffering like her.

Looters had gutted every building in downtown Dobani Proper.

Shopkeepers stood dazed, standing outside their destroyed buildings. One store was on fire, but no aid came. The streets were empty aside from a few stragglers; patrolling soldiers rushed them away under the guise of making it home for curfew.

Up ahead, a bent old man struggled to cross the street. Pearla headed that way, finally reaching him and offering him her arm. The old man took it gratefully.

His cane clicked on the pavement, followed by a few grunts of pain, but otherwise, he didn't make a sound. When Pearla led him successfully across the street, he gave her a toothless grin of thanks. The man's eyes were milky-white; he was nearly blind.

Pearla turned to make her way back to the transport and ran right into a soldier. He was tall, his shoulders wide. He held a rifle across his chest. "Where are you going with that merchandise?" he asked her.

Pearla's arms tightened around the bundle of clothes. If she and her family were leaving Dobani, and she was certain they had to, they would need supplies. "These are mine," she told him plainly. "I was just on my way home."

The soldier scowled. He reached out, edging the clothes with the muzzle of his gun. "These still have tags on them. All merchandise belongs to the government now."

Pearla said nothing. She held them closer to her body, as if they could protect her from his threatening manner.

"Give them to me," he said. And then he pointed the gun right at her belly. "I'm not asking."

Her lips trembled. She instinctively curved her body, shielding her baby. Lorien kicked against her ribs…a protest, a plea, and Pearla's breath hitched. More soldiers joined him. There was nowhere to go.

Suddenly, seemingly from nowhere, she heard the crack of a cane. The old man from before, the one she'd helped across the street, assaulted the soldier with all the strength he could muster. "You would point a gun at a pregnant woman? Point the gun at me!"

The soldier turned. Other soldiers who had joined grabbed the old man, stretching him between them. The soldier who had threatened Pearla hit the old man with the butt of his gun, and he crumpled between them.

Pearla cried out. She saw the cane hit the sidewalk, rolling into the gutter. Pearla turned and ran with all the speed she could gather. The transport was in sight. She'd almost reached it. Then came the shot—sharp and final. Another followed. Her hand shook on the door of the transport, and she climbed inside.

Pearla sped off, not even noticing where she was going. She had to get away. She had to get home.

Her hands were shaking. The road blurred. Only when a sob tore from her throat did she realize she was crying.

CHAPTER 6

The drive seemed to go on forever. She took care not to drive too fast, but she was desperate to get home. Her mind was racing. Dobani had changed. There was no going back now.

On either side of the highway stood stores, gutted and shuttered. People were lining the streets in a mass exodus, loaded with only the belongings they could carry. Distant flames lit the sky; the smell of black smoke wafted in through the transport ventilation system, nearly choking her.

Pearla moved her hand from the wheel and placed it over her stomach. Her baby would never know the Dobani she grew up with…the one she was born on. It would never know the generosity and kindness of the people, the safety and security of its land.

She wiped a stray tear. It would know love. It would know safety, even if it was the last thing she did.

◆ ◆ ◆

Phoenix paced, his mind racing. He had read the note Pearla left, as sparse as it was. There had been an emergency at the store, and she had to go. Phoenix had tried her on the holopad multiple times, but to no avail. She was unreachable.

Visions of Pearla stranded on the road alone flashed in front of his eyes. Pearla hurt…injured. Needing him. His hands twitched. He grabbed his jacket and headed toward the door.

"Daddy, she'll be home any minute. I know it. Now is not the time to separate."

Phoenix realized his daughter's hand was on his arm. He tried to calm himself, to think reasonably. But internally, he knew the dangers that lurked beyond their doors. He knew what was at stake.

He reached for Sev's hand and covered it with his own. "You're right, of course. Try calling her again, hmm? Maybe it will go through."

Sev nodded, a soft smile on her face. "We're going to get through this, you know. All four of us."

Phoenix's eyes filled with tears. She'd counted the baby. Of course she had.

Just then, there was the sound of tires crunching on rocky soil, the low hum of a transport engine. Phoenix ran outside to see Pearla opening the door of the transport and getting out.

His breath rushed out of him, nearly doubling him over. The relief at seeing her whole and unharmed washed over him, leaving him struggling for words. "Drek be praised," he managed to whisper. He approached and wrapped his arms around her. "I was so worried, Pearl. I was out of my mind with it."

Pearla took a shaky breath, finally looking up at him. Phoenix could tell by her face that something was terribly wrong. Her eyes were puffy, and her fair complexion was even paler than usual.

"Pearl?" He clutched her tighter, suddenly afraid she might collapse. She seemed exhausted.

Sev ran out into the yard, her eyes wide. Phoenix watched as she took in the two of them. Pearla clung to Phoenix like a woman lost at sea…shaking, breathless, undone. She looked as though her legs were ready to buckle.

"Let's get you inside," Phoenix said gravely. With Sev's help on the other side, they led Pearla inside the house and lowered her onto the couch. She sat down gingerly, and Sev wrapped a blanket around her shoulders.

Phoenix wet a cloth with cool water and rushed to her side. He wiped her face tenderly, smoothing away the tear tracks and smudges of dirt on her cheek.

"What happened, my love? Tell me everything. Why did you run off without me this morning?"

Pearla caught his hand, the artificial one, and gave it a gentle squeeze. She gave Sev a furtive glance, then averted her eyes. "It's gone," she whispered. "It's all gone."

Sev leaned in, her hands on her knees where she sat across from them. "What do you mean by that, Pearla? What's gone?"

Pearla met her gaze, eyes glittering. "My shop," she managed hoarsely. "The soldiers raided it. Told people to take what they wanted." Her voice hardened. "Said they'd need it where they were going."

Phoenix blew out a breath. He instinctively pulled her to him, cradling her gently. All his previous ire at her hasty exit without him faded under the evidence of her grief. He rubbed his hand over her back until she had fully relaxed, until he could feel the tension leach from her shoulders.

She pulled away from him, looking at Phoenix, then at Sev. "People are leaving," she said. "I think we need to, too."

Phoenix blinked, unbelieving things had gotten so bad. "Perhaps the Enforcers can help. Maybe if we call them—"

Pearla shook her head. "There are no Enforcers. Only soldiers. And they aren't helping anyone. They're not protecting us." She glanced between them, her gaze restless. "I'm not entirely convinced they're from Dobani."

She lowered her head, apparently hesitant to say what came next. A full shudder went through her. "One pulled a gun on me," she murmured without looking up. "Pointed it right at the baby."

Sev gasped, and Phoenix's ears rang. His body felt tight as a bowstring. He clenched his fists at his sides, feeling anger coursing through his muscles, calling him to action.

They could've killed her, he thought wildly. *They still could*. Pearla was in danger…the baby…Sev. They couldn't stay here.

He took a few calming breaths through his nose, trying to quell his wrath. He needed to think, needed to act, not just feel.

"We go," he said finally. Sev was watching him with a hand to her mouth. Pearla said nothing; she sat looking straight ahead, lost in thought. He turned to Pearla. "Your parents still have that place in the Highlands? We'll hide out there for a few days until we can figure out what to do next."

Pearla nodded. "It could work," she said. "They haven't been in years, but they never sold it. If you don't mind bunking with the sheep; they're used to coming in and out."

Sev laughed, breaking the tension. "I love sheep. Sounds like heaven to me."

Phoenix's mouth quirked into a tight smile. "We leave by daybreak. Pack light…only what will fit in the transport." He regarded Sev, his eyes sad. "I'm sorry, little mouse. I know this is hard. But we've got each other. That's what matters most."

She walked over to him, giving him a brief hug. "We'll be home wherever we are, Daddy. As long as we're together. Try not to worry."

She released him and strolled off toward her room. Phoenix heard the door shut. He'd raised an incredible daughter, he thought. A strong young woman. She amazed him every day.

Pearla cast a furtive glance in his direction, her eyes heavy. "Phoenix, I'm so sorry for leaving without you," she murmured. "I didn't think. I didn't want to wake you, and—"

He kissed her hair, then smoothed it with his hand. "It's alright, love. We're together now. And we're staying that way. Have to keep her safe."

Phoenix grinned; his insistence that the baby was a girl was a running joke between them. He could feel her huff, then bury her face against him.

He withdrew, looking at her. "We'll have to pack for the baby, too." He swallowed, realizing what that meant. "We don't know when we'll get to come back."

She understood his meaning, tension clouding her features. He felt her curl her fingers into his shirt, saw her furrowed brow. He knew she must realize she wouldn't have the baby at home. It was a sobering prospect.

"I used to summer in the Highlands," she said with finality. "We can welcome the baby there."

Phoenix stood, holding out a hand for Pearla. "Come love. There's much to do before tomorrow, and we'll need a little sleep, to boot."

CHAPTER 7

Sev was up before everyone. Her meager bag sat on her bed, ready at a moment's notice. She'd turned off the fairy lights in her room, the lamp near the window. All was still and dark in the early morning light.

She wandered out into the hall, and she saw that the light in the nursery was on. She peeked inside. Pearla was sitting in the rocking chair within, looking out the window. She had a tiny onesie in her hands.

Pearla saw her before she could sneak away and waved her in.

Sev walked over to Pearla; the sun was just coming up and streaming through the baby's window. Her father had built it to resemble hers, with a cushioned bench and pillows on the sill.

Pearla gazed at the tiny suit, running her hands over the soft fabric. "The baby might never see this room," Pearla mused. Sev watched her face; it was still…peaceful. She seemed sad, but she hadn't been crying.

"You don't know that," Sev said. "They may. We are leaving, but nothing says we can't come back."

Pearla smiled a little sadly and closed her eyes. "Perhaps," she said, but Sev doubted she believed it.

Sev kneeled beside her. Upon closer inspection, she saw Pearla holding the blue calcet…the baby's gift. "Keep this for now," Pearla told her. "Cards aren't working. It may be the only currency we have."

Sev gave her a tight nod, took it and put it away in her pack. "We won't need to use it, Pearla. But I'll keep it. Just in case."

Pearla reached out and traced Sev's face with her hand. "I hope the baby grows up to be just like you," she said fondly. "So strong. So capable and loving."

Sev felt her eyes sting, but she blinked the tears away. She laid her head on Pearla's lap. They remained there for a long time, Pearla stroking over Sev's hair. Sev realized, then, the gravity of the moment. They were leaving home. Maybe forever.

◆ ◆ ◆

The transport idled in the front yard. He had packed the compartment as full as it would get. Most of the things were for the baby…supplies they might need. He didn't know how advanced the Highlands were or if you could even buy things for babies there. He had to be prepared…it's all that mattered.

Sev came up beside him and grabbed his hand. The sun was coming up over the palms. Her eyes fixed on the distant horizon…her beach and the water.

"I'm going to miss this," she breathed. "I found my peace here." She looked up at him, her eyes damp. "We both did."

He wrapped his prosthetic arm around her…the one he never wanted until she did. She had always brought out the very best in him, his Sev. He felt her grief at the loss of their home. It was the same as his.

Behind them, Pearla came walking out of the house. It was dark behind her; all the lights were off. She carried a small bag…Phoenix had forbidden her from carrying anything heavy. She passed them and approached the transport, tossing her carryon in the back. Pearla looked back at them, a determined set to her mouth.

"Ready?"

Phoenix gripped Sev's shoulder, then relaxed his hand. Sev studied him, a soft smile on her face. She was no longer crying. She appeared resolved, almost hopeful. "Yeah," she said. "We're ready."

They loaded up and pulled out of the driveway. Phoenix noticed his neighbor was already gone, his house boarded up. He'd plowed up his garden; stray vegetables he hadn't stored or taken with him lay wasting in the yard.

Phoenix swallowed. He had packed food, but not enough for the long term. He was relying on the Highlands to have fertile land…a robust economy. Maybe he was putting too much faith in a place he'd never been, but what choice did they have?

The rural roads unfurled into the city. Phoenix witnessed firsthand the destruction Pearla had seen, the cause of her alarm. In the back seat, he could see Sev watching silently, clearly stricken.

Pearla said nothing. She stared straight ahead, lost in thought. Distracted as he was by the chaos and carnage surrounding them, Pearla saw it first.

"Phoenix?"

Sev peered ahead, over her father's shoulder. Phoenix could smell the tang of exhaust, could hear the orders over the loudspeaker up ahead. He recognized the military vehicles as the same type he'd seen in town, only this time, there were even more of them. Abandoned transports sat scattered, some still idling. In the distance, the military had rounded up everyone into two groups.

Fear nearly blinded him. They could not go this way. They had to turn back.

But it was too late. A car slammed into them suddenly, sending Pearla and Sev bracing against their safety restraints. The collision moved the transport a few feet, bottle-necking traffic. They had nowhere to go.

Phoenix was breathless and shaky as he took stock of himself. He snapped his head around to Pearla, eyes roving over her. "Are you ok?" He caught his daughter's frightened face in the mirror. "Sev, what about you?"

"I'm fine," Pearla breathed. The crash had shaken her, but she appeared whole. Sev nodded, then uttered a tight "me too" just loud enough for her father to hear.

They couldn't turn around. They couldn't go through. The collision had trapped them in traffic, stuck between transports and a military blockade.

Phoenix looked at his family, assessing their frightened eyes. He had to do something. They couldn't just sit here.

"Let's get out, girls. Take what you can. Leave the rest. We'll go on foot. See if we can get around it."

Pearla's eyes grew wide. "How far are we going to get on foot?" she said, her voice laced with panic.

Phoenix frowned. "I don't know. But we don't have a choice." He turned to Sev. "Mouse? Get your pack. Let's go."

They opened the door of the crippled transport. Phoenix led Pearla and Sev to the side of the road. There was a tall fence off the sidewalk up ahead; if they could get behind it somehow, they could make it past the blockade unnoticed.

They walked for a mile, maybe more. Phoenix felt vulnerable…exposed. The fence was insight, but still very far away. He was running out of options, and he was already out of time.

Just then, he heard a soldier call to another group. "Them, walking there! Get them in line with the others."

Oh, Drek, he thought miserably. There was nowhere to go…nowhere to hide. He gripped Pearla's hand, trying to reassure her, but he was terrified himself.

Two soldiers stopped them just feet from the fence. One was stocky and imposing; the other was about Phoenix's build. The stocky one motioned to them with his rifle. "Get in line with the others."

Pearla glanced nervously at Phoenix, unsure of what to do. Sev stepped between them, her face twisted with rage. "Why should we?" she snapped. She had her fists balled in anger, her body rigid.

The stocky soldier narrowed his eyes. He grabbed her arm, and Sev cried out. "Because I *said so*, little girl," he said gruffly.

Phoenix pushed the soldier off. "Don't lay your hands on my daughter again. I don't care who you are."

It enraged him. The stocky soldier stepped back on his foot and pointed the rifle right at Phoenix's chest. Pearla screamed. Sev stood by speechless and terrified.

The other soldier stepped in front of the rifle. "Lars, don't. Why don't you take a break, huh? I'll handle them."

The stocky soldier cursed under his breath but eventually lowered his rifle. "Hope it's worth you risking your neck for this off-worlder scum," he muttered. The soldier waited until the man had stalked away before he turned toward them.

Phoenix was shaking, though he tried to hide it. His muscles trembled…adrenaline flooded his bloodstream. *That was close*, he thought bleakly. He had to be more careful.

The soldier left studied them, and his posture softened. He lowered his face covering. Phoenix gasped. He was very young, no older than Sev.

"I'm sorry," he said. "Lars has a temper."

Pearla gaped at him, her eyes wide. "You're just a child," she murmured.

The man pressed his mouth into a line. "Eighteen this month. Ma'am."

Phoenix could feel the fear recede, and he chanced a step toward him. "Let us go, son. Please. My wife is going to have a baby."

Pearla eyed him sharply; they were not married. She had thought about it, admittedly, especially with the baby coming, but they had never discussed it.

The soldier's eyes flitted to Pearla's round belly, to Sev, and then back to Phoenix. His gaze was empathetic, but something changed.

"I can't," he said, his voice shaking. "You've got to get in line with the others. You'll do it, or—or I'll have to shoot you."

Phoenix swallowed. He spread his hands. "You don't want to do that. You're a good person. I can tell. Not like these others."

The soldier glanced away. His eyes snagged on Sev; then he shut them.

With a steadying breath, he raised the gun.

"I'm sorry," he repeated. "Get in line now. With everyone else."

Pearla instinctively covered her stomach, and beside him, Sev flinched. Phoenix felt his heart sink. He gave his girls an affirming nod, fighting the tremble in his throat. Sev's arm was red where the other soldier had grabbed her. He felt bile rise in his throat.

The soldier led them at gunpoint to the group at the back of the line. Women held their crying babies, swaddled in little more than rags. He closed his eyes. He couldn't imagine his child being brought into this world the way it was now.

Sev grabbed her father's hand and looked up at him. He could tell she was thinking the same thing.

They had to do something, Phoenix thought wildly. They had to act. If they ushered them onto that transport, there was no telling where they might end up.

Dead, a little voice whispered, and he shut his eyes against it.

The soldier turned. Phoenix's hands twitched, itching to do something. He stepped forward to strike him…to take his chance. Before he could act, a woman beside them broke and ran. The stocky soldier stepped forward, ordering her to stop. She didn't. He shot her. She fell to the ground with a cry.

People in the crowd screamed, and soldiers bellowed at them to keep the order. Phoenix could feel Pearla trembling beside him…could feel Sev's shocked silence filling the spaces between them.

There was no choice but to obey. If he wanted them to get out alive, they had to comply.

CHAPTER 8

They'd stood in line for hours, forced into silence by the soldiers' guns. The children standing with their parents whimpered, tired from standing on their feet for so long. Others sighed in desperation or sniffed miserably to keep the tears at bay. Still, some trembled quietly, unable to process the crippling fear of what was taking place.

Phoenix was worried about Pearla. Her feet swelled even after a day spent in her shop. He knew she was suffering now. He pressed her to him, and she leaned into his touch. A small exhale was the only sign she was uncomfortable.

The soldiers had taken their belongings…all their supplies for the baby Phoenix had carefully packed in the transport. They had nothing but the clothes on their backs now. Sev still had her pack; miraculously, it had gone undisturbed.

Sev shifted on her feet; Phoenix's throat tightened at the sight of her sunburned cheeks. There was no shade, and although they were at the onset of the off-season, the sun was bright and blistering. She peered up at him with doleful eyes, her mouth turned down in a soft frown. It broke his heart to see his girls suffering so.

Sometime later, the line moved. It was about four people across, and so long Phoenix couldn't see the end. Up ahead, it curved. Soldiers were loading people onto trucks.

Fear sliced through him. He gripped Pearla's hand, then Sev's. "We stay together," he breathed. "Whatever you do, don't let go."

They squeezed back, showing they understood. A few steps later, Pearla made a small noise beside him, then covered her belly with her hand. He looked over, and she was smiling to herself, her eyes closed. Phoenix realized the baby must've moved.

The line bled into the cold shadow of the military transport trucks. They were huge, armored vehicles with wooden bench seats. Phoenix watched as soldiers on either side of the hatch pushed people inside, pressing the butt of their rifles into their backs. He clutched Pearla to him and pushed Sev behind him. If the soldiers pushed anyone, it would be him.

It was Phoenix's turn. He stopped at the hatch and considered the soldier to his right. He resembled the young man from before; his eyes were the same.

"Let me help her on…please. She's with child."

He could feel Sev's hand wrap around his upper arm, fingers pressing tightly. The soldier waffled, clearly weighing his answer.

"Fine," he finally said. He eyed Sev, and his gaze seemed to soften for a moment. "Help them both on. But be quick about it."

Relief flooded through him. He wasted no time boosting Pearla, then Sev, onto the transport. Pearla took a seat on the bench within, and the relief on her face was obvious.

The young soldier gave Phoenix a rough push through the hatch, but Phoenix said nothing. He'd let him help Pearla and Sev, and for that, he was grateful. Phoenix fell onto the dusty floor of the transport with a grunt, and Sev helped him get to his feet.

He brushed himself off and settled on the bench between them. It was sweltering and stale inside, the air rife with too many sweaty bodies and the pungent tang of fear. Every inhale was a labor. Phoenix could feel the sweat bead on his forehead, the lack of ventilation within drawing it out of his pores.

He took Sev's hair, gone long now, and pulled it away from her collar. He laid his hand against her neck, squeezing gently. "Thanks, Daddy," she whispered. Her neck was dewy and warm.

Others murmured among themselves. The soldiers did not seem to mind. Pearla grabbed Phoenix's arm weakly. She was pale, her face devoid of color save for the spots of heat high on her cheekbones.

"I don't feel very good," she breathed. "My ears are ringing."

Phoenix stood, and a soldier immediately trained their weapon on him. "Sit down," the soldier ordered. The voice was female.

His pulse hammered in his head, and he felt lightheaded from the heat. *Would she shoot?* He knew what happened when people became desperate…what moved them to violence. It didn't take much.

"She needs water," Phoenix said. He did not sit down. "Please help her."

The female soldier held the gun on him, her eyes above her face covering impassive and cold. Sev stood next to her father. She was shaking.

"What good are we to you if we're dead?! What is all of this for, anyway? Why won't anyone tell us anything?"

The other people packed in the transport mumbled their agreement. There was not one person who wasn't sweaty, red-faced, and miserable.

The soldier shot over Sev's head, the bullet exiting the back of the transport and leaving a small hole behind. "Next time, I won't miss," she said menacingly.

The people inside quieted. Sev said nothing else, but she remained on her feet. So did Phoenix.

It felt like a last stand. Phoenix determined that wherever they were going, nothing good awaited them, no matter what the government said. Something needed to be done. Pearla needed water. He would not relent.

Beside him, Pearla tugged at his shirt. "No, Phoenix. Not like this," she protested. Her voice was raspy and dry.

"Give her the water!" someone else shouted. He was a man about Phoenix's age. "Have you forgotten what Dobani stands for? How we treat each other?"

A few other voices joined her, and the soldier finally lowered her weapon.

She went over to the corner and withdrew a canteen. The woman gave it to Phoenix, who handed it to Pearla. She accepted it and took a few shaky sips. "Thank you," she whispered.

Phoenix watched Pearla take the water, saw the way her hand trembled. Her chest was heaving. She needed a medic. She needed air. He almost said as much, but then he remembered the one in line, the one who'd broken and run. The one who they'd shot for her defiance. He tamped down the desire to say more, but it wasn't easy.

Sev and Phoenix finally sat, but he did not stop looking at the soldier until the transport finally started moving.

Where to, he still didn't know.

◆ ◆ ◆

Sev and Pearla slept on either side of Phoenix, their heads resting against him. The transport had no viewpanes. Once the hatch was closed, it was pitch black, except for what light leaked in through the cracks in the paneled walls. It was hot and dusty. The roar of the engines reverberated through the lumbering transport.

When it finally came to a stop, the female soldier began parsing them into groups. She went row by row, moving the men to one side, the women to the other. People screamed and cried. She split the children among family members, causing tearful outbursts.

Sev watched Pearla. She had her hand over her belly, and the pulse in her neck was fluttering rapidly. They could not lose each other, Sev thought. They would never make it alone.

Phoenix, Sev, and Pearla all held hands, standing close together despite the heat. The soldier came to their row and paused. Pearla met her eyes. "Do you have a family?" she asked her quietly.

The woman said nothing for a moment, then reluctantly, she nodded.

"Then don't separate us," she said, her voice tinged with desperation. "Just don't."

The woman looked at Pearla, then at Sev. Finally, she glanced at Phoenix before finally walking to the next row.

Pearla exhaled shakily and tightened her hold on Phoenix's hand. Sev watched them both, a small amount of relief easing her chest. They were still together. Everything would be fine if they had each other.

They stumbled out of the transport and ended up in front of a large warehouse. More soldiers waved them in. These people did not have guns, Pearla noticed. They did not wear face coverings. An older soldier offered her a gentle smile. It seemed out of place, given all they had been through.

As they stepped into the warehouse, the roar of engines and crying children faded behind them. The air was still thick with, but the absence of shouting soldiers made it feel unnaturally quiet. The people hesitated, glancing at each other, uncertain of what lay beyond.

Once inside the warehouse, the soldiers cordoned them off by numbered sections…they did not allow them to reunite with their families. Those whom the soldiers had separated on the transport wailed for want of their loved ones, their cries reverberating off the walls of the warehouse. It made Sev hold on to Phoenix and Pearla even tighter.

After they'd settled, uniformed workers came around with ration bars and bottles of water. There were cots in the warehouse, and bathrooms, but few other amenities. Still, the rations and water were welcome after so long without.

Sev chewed her ration and swallowed it quickly, as if someone might take it from her. An early life of hard survival had activated old instincts. She eyed her father, her gaze sharp. "What do we do, Daddy?" she whispered. "What's our next steps?"

Phoenix drank half his water, then gave the other half to Pearla to add to hers. She tried to stop him, but he insisted. His mouth tightened into a line; his brow furrowed. Sev could see him working through the options, trying to find the best way forward.

"We find out what's going on," he said. "We talk to people, now that we can. I know someone knows something."

Sev nodded, already finished with her bar. Her stomach no longer cramped with hunger and thirst, but the fear of the unknown was overwhelming. She glanced over at Pearla. She was still very pale, and though the ventilation was better in the warehouse, she was sweating.

"You need to rest, Pearla. You don't look well."

Phoenix observed her then. Sev could see the worry on his face.

"I'll go see who I can find…maybe someone I know," Sev said. "You two sit tight." She stood and dusted her clothes. "I love you," she told them before weaving through the tight rows of displaced citizens.

She looked back, and Phoenix and Pearla were watching her go. They seemed tired…already beaten down, her father worried nearly beyond recognition. Sev suspected the hardships were just beginning. Dobani had betrayed them, stripped them of their freedom.

But Sev had never been that easy to pin down.

CHAPTER 9

Phoenix didn't sleep. He stared up at the seemingly endless ceiling of the warehouse and watched industrial-sized fans turn lazily in the humid air. Pearla slept fitfully to his right, curled on her side. Sev was to his left.

She'd returned from her fact-finding mission tight-lipped and frustrated, her silence more telling than words. No one knew anything, or they weren't talking. A few hours of brooding and she'd finally drifted off, but her rest had been fitful. She murmured in her sleep—plagued by old nightmares or by recent horrors; he didn't know.

Phoenix was aware, with so many people grouped together and desperate, that it was a recipe for violence. He kept watch, eyes trained on the ceiling, but his senses alert. If anyone so much as moved in their direction, he would know it.

The fans groaned on frozen joints, wafting stale air to the floor of the warehouse. Phoenix was not the only one awake. He could feel the shifty eyes on them, could hear the moans and sighs of the sick and very young. Some people were talking quietly a few rows down, and he covertly turned in that direction.

There were four of them huddled together, their heads bent. They spoke lowly in near unison; sometimes their voices would raise enough for Phoenix to make out a word or two, and it piqued his interest.

At least…a plan. Can't make our move…wait until we get there.

Phoenix's eyes widened. If they were making plans, he needed to know about them. If he offered his help, maybe they would include his family, too. He made note of their faces, one by one, committing them to memory. Just in case.

He closed his eyes—just for a moment, he told himself. Just to rest before it all broke loose. The drone of the fans faded, and the warehouse darkened behind his lids.

◆ ◆ ◆

They awoke to a loud buzzer. It was not yet daylight.

Sev blinked awake, the illusion of sleep still clinging to her consciousness. For a split second, she thought she might be at home in her bed. Pearla was in the kitchen, making stim brew. Her father sat in his chair reading the holopages. After breakfast, she would go to the beach and brown in the sun until lunch.

But she wasn't at home. She bolted upright, reality falling into place around her like pieces of a mismatched puzzle. To her right, her father was tending to Pearla, helping her sit upright on the cot. His hair stood up in all directions, and dark circles ringed his eyes. He clearly hadn't slept.

The buzzer sounded again. All around her, people began rising from the cots, stretching stiff bodies and murmuring amongst themselves. Sev watched as uniformed workers filed out, pushing carts of ration bars and water. *Breakfast of champions*, Sev thought, eyeing the bar like it might bite first.

She nudged her father. "Hey Daddy? You ok?"

He gave her his usual lopsided smile. His hand went out to caress her cheek, skin rough but warm against her face. "Right as rain, little mouse," he said, but his heart wasn't in it. She covered his hand where it lay against her face and gave it a little squeeze.

Pearla was worse than her father. She was ashen, her face thin. Her eyes appeared sunken from poor sleep. Sev glanced up, and a uniformed worker pushing a cart was standing over them. He had a blank stare and a creepy, pasted-on smile. He handed each of them a water bottle and a ration bar. "Good morning!" he said in a faux-chipper demeanor.

"Nothing good about it," someone grumbled to Sev's left, and her mouth quirked up in a smile. She watched as the man's smile faltered a little before he moved on.

She popped the cap on the water bottle and brought it to her lips. Phoenix haltered her.

"Do you think it's ok to drink? Or the ration bar? They wouldn't drug us, would they?"

Pearla gasped. "For Drek's sake," she whispered, horrified.

Sev considered. "We all ate them last night. Drank the water. I feel fine."

He nodded. "Ok then, mouse. I just…I don't know who to trust anymore. Certainly not them."

Sev considered that. She took a swig of water. It cooled her throat and cleared a little of the dust that had settled there.

To Pearla's right, an old woman leaned forward. "Here, sweetheart. Take mine. For the babe."

She held out her ration bar in a gnarled, arthritic hand. Her face was kind, open. It reminded her of all this world had lost. The goodness of the people.

Pearla held up her hand. "I couldn't, ma'am," she said. "You need to eat."

The woman just shook her head and placed it on the edge of Pearla's cot. She straightened as best she could. "They say there's a war."

It immediately caught Sev's attention. This was the first she'd heard of war, of any kind of reason this was happening. She peered at her, silently encouraging the woman to continue.

"The Dobani Military is taking us somewhere safe, so we won't get hurt. Isn't that lovely?"

Beside her, Phoenix huffed. "I can take care of myself and my family, ma'am. And we should have the choice to do so."

Sev nodded. "He's right. We can fend for ourselves if we choose. It's not fair."

The old woman just smiled and turned away, seemingly oblivious to their anger.

Sev leaned toward her father. "Do you think she knows what she's talking about, Dad? You think there's a war? That this is an evacuation of some sort?"

Before he could answer her, another buzzer sounded. In the middle of the warehouse, a soldier stood on a raised platform. He had a bullhorn in his hand.

"Gather your belongings. Evacuation to Kedros will commence imminently."

Shocked voices traveled through the crowd like a wave. Gasps, then open shouts of outrage. Phoenix narrowed his eyes, glancing at Sev. "Kedros? The moon?"

Dread settled in her veins. There was nothing on Kedros. It was a barren land, barely viable. Dobani had sent its garbage there to be incinerated for years.

"They're throwing us away like trash," Sev muttered to herself. Beside Phoenix, Pearla was crying.

"My baby's going to be born in a garbage dump," she whimpered. Phoenix wrapped his arms around her, shushing her quietly.

He met Sev's eyes. There was defiance there, but also a trace of dread.

◆ ◆ ◆

Barely an hour later, the soldiers rounded them up and divided them into two lines. They allowed families to reunite briefly, the only comfort. Phoenix, Sev, and Pearla stood pressed together, holding on to each other's clothes so they would not be separated.

The line moved out of the warehouse and into the midday Dobani sun. It was cooler outside, the off-season sending northern breezes down to the coast.

The space transports hovered about a half mile away, their hulking hulls battered and dull.

They were headed for Kedros, Sev thought with despair. There was nothing she could do.

She thought briefly of her friends at school, their neighbors. *Was this happening to them, too?* It made her unbelievably sad.

Phoenix must've sensed her heartache, because he reached for her hand and gave it a little squeeze. His eyes transmitted silent assurance and, above everything, love. It made her feel somewhat better.

Boarding the space transports was a much more orderly affair than it had been boarding the trucks. The soldiers seemed less cruel and more detached, a change Sev would take any day.

In another line, the old woman from before gave them a gentle wave, a soft smile. Sev hoped she would be ok; no one was with her, from what she could tell, and she was clearly deluded about the military's intentions.

Sev sighed. She couldn't help her any more than she could help herself, now.

The inside of the transport was little more than a great open space. There were no seats…no restraints. They settled on the floor, Pearla with great difficulty, given her advanced pregnancy. The viewport above them was round, little more than a porthole. The milky light from its dirty glass shone onto the floor in front of them. There was otherwise no other illumination.

After everyone had boarded and packed tightly within the transport, the hatch closed, leaving them in semi-darkness. It was still within, the air inside rank. Some people cried. Children, all out of tears, sniffed quietly on their parents' shoulders. The engines roared to life, and the transport took off, headed to Kedros.

Sev rose to her knees to look out of the viewport. Other transports took off behind them, a sinister ballet. Dobani shrank, a green and brown mass of land, little more than a hand-width. The silver expanse of the ocean blinked out of view.

Sev had a terrible feeling that it was the last time she would ever see it.

CHAPTER 10

Space was cold, as usual; the dark void seemed to suck every bit of warmth from her body whenever she was in it. Even as a child, being in the Black with Del for days on end, space had felt like a foreign invader…something ominous and oppressive.

Sitting on the floor of the transport didn't help. The steel riveted floor, the solid walls. She shivered, her limbs like ice.

Sev looked around. It was nighttime back on Dobani. Most people were asleep, huddling together against the cold. Others stared wide-eyed into the dark; the only light in the transport was the pall of a distant moon, the glow of stars outside.

She noticed a girl, maybe a little younger, leaning against a woman. She had her knees pulled up to her chest. Sev's gaze snagged on her, and they locked eyes briefly.

The girl gave her a little wave, nothing more than the waggle of fingers, and Sev returned it. Sev realized then that she knew her…had seen her in the dining hall at school.

She wondered briefly if the girl even recognized her, given all that had happened. Was it just yesterday that they were in school together?

Things would never be the same. She knew that now.

Phoenix sat right next to her, his arms around Pearla. He'd finally succumbed to sleep; she didn't think he had slept at all since all of this started.

Pearla slept too, her stark white face glowing in the starlight.

Sev was afraid.

There was no telling what awaited them on Kedros, or how long they would be there. If Dobani really was at war, they could be there for months, maybe even years. The loss of their life on Dobani settled beneath Sev's ribs, a hollow ache.

She leaned against her father. The warmth of his back leached into her skin, reminding her of sunny days on the beach…of the safety and security of her bed back home.

Sev closed her eyes. The transport rumbled around them, shaking her bones. Her mind drifted to a now faraway world of crystalline waters and toasted sand. It was the last thing she thought of before sleep finally claimed her.

◆ ◆ ◆

Phoenix awoke, taking stock of his stiffened limbs, of Pearla and Sev asleep against him. The transport was preparing to land; he could tell by the familiar swoop of his stomach, the sudden turbulence.

He nudged Sev gently, immediately regretting waking her. She wore a deep frown, even in sleep, and her brow furrowed.

Sev blinked up at him, her eyes unfocused. "What's wrong, Daddy?"

But he could see realization dawn on her as soon as she asked the question. She sat up straighter, pulling her knees against her chest. Without restraints, they'd need to brace themselves.

"We're almost there," Phoenix whispered, though he didn't need to. She nodded, and he brushed the hair away from her face. It'd come loose from her ponytail, and there was a smudge of dirt on her cheek.

"I need a shower," she groused. Her cheeks burned red, ashamed of her bedraggled state. Phoenix huffed. "That makes two of us." He thumbed over the apple of her cheek, and she leaned into his touch. "Still my beautiful little girl, though."

Sev's mouth softened. "I hope we make it, Daddy. I'm worried."

He moved his hand to her chin and nudged it, so she looked at him fully. Her eyes were wide and luminous in the atmospheric light from the viewport.

"We're going to be alright, little mouse. You hear your old man? I'm not going to let anything happen to you, Pearla, or little Lorien."

Sev smiled then. "Ok," she breathed.

He turned, and Pearla was stretching awake. "We're landing soon, dear heart. Stay close to me."

A few moments later, the cold dissipated. A bright flash of light sparked in the viewpane—the fire from reentry. The transport shook, and the air became thick with ozone. People gasped and cried out, clutching each other. He could tell many had never been off world, were unfamiliar with landing procedures, and his heart went out to them.

Phoenix put his arms around both Pearla and Sev. They put their heads down, eyes closed, and tried to make themselves as small as possible.

Some terrifying minutes later, the transport landed on the surface, and the engines powered down.

They sat there in silence, listening to the cooling engines tick, the pops and whirs of the huge transport settling on the surface. The landing had stunned most into silence, and there was only the occasional sniff or stifled cry and the intermittent restless wail of a baby.

The hatch fell open with a loud shuddering sound, and dusty grey light poured into the transport. Soldiers filed in, ordering Dobani citizens into three lines.

Phoenix watched, horrified, as soldiers divided the people. Families became separated…people screamed and cried. A few fought back, kicking and punching just to be hit over the head with the butt of a rifle.

He looked at Sev, then at Pearla. The fear in their eyes was palpable, and he felt instantly responsible for it.

Phoenix squeezed Sev's shoulder, looking from one to the other. Sev blinked away tears, and Pearla trembled. "We'll find each other again," he told them. "I swear it."

A soldier pulled him away, into another line. His shoulders stiffened…his fists balled at his sides, itching to act. He turned to the soldier, pleading with his eyes. "Don't take me away from them," he whispered, but the man ignored him. A muscle ticked in his jaw, and he gritted his teeth.

Phoenix turned just in time to see Sev being pushed into a line to the far left of the transport. Her eyes were stricken, her shoulders rigid. Pearla was in the middle line, openly crying.

Pearla reached toward him, but a soldier blocked her path. "Please—" she cried, but the soldier turned away.

Phoenix had never felt angrier. He had never felt more helpless. His stomach roiled, and his eyes burned with frustrated tears.

◆ ◆ ◆

Sev watched her father in line, memorizing who he stood beside. The soldiers moved their lines out into the murky sky of Kedros. No one spoke. A few people cried. Sev did neither. She held her head up, swallowing her grief, rage, and fear.

Kedros was a grey world, with a dusty granite-colored surface and perpetual twilight. There were rows and rows of tents and low buildings, all as bland as this monochromatic world appeared to be. The soldiers directed their lines to join with others, and Sev quickly realized they were separating them by age and gender.

She had lost sight of her father, but she kept her eyes on Pearla. She had her head down, both hands on her stomach. Her salt-chapped face was tear-streaked and puffy.

They led all the women in Sev's group into a large tent. There were cots there, but no pillows or blankets. Once they'd settled, a uniformed woman entered, bullhorn in hand. She had a serious face, her hair up in a severe bun.

"Welcome to Kedros," the woman intoned, her voice anything but welcoming. "This is a temporary arrangement, organized by the Dobani government to keep you safe."

The woman had a scar across her cheek and a menacing aura. Murmurs went up from the group of women, hushed whispers. Sev scanned the faces there, trying to find Pearla. She'd gotten lost in the crowd.

"Sleep tonight. You will get your work assignments tomorrow."

And with that, she was gone.

Sev eyed the other women, schooling her features to keep them impassive. *Work assignments? If they were refugees from a war, why were they having to work?* None of it made sense.

Suddenly, the lights went out in the tent, and Sev got the hint. She settled as best she could on the cot. She thought of Pearla; the poor thing must be scared and uncomfortable, as pregnant as she was.

And she thought of her father. He was under so much stress, she knew, to keep their family together. He must feel terrible now.

But she would find him. She would find Pearla, too. No force in this world—or any other—would keep her from her family.

CHAPTER 11

Phoenix lay awake, unable to sleep. Kedros was wet and dark, the steady patter of rain on the roof of the men's tent a metronome of misery.

He missed his family.

Phoenix turned on his side. He'd left his arm on, half afraid someone might steal it in the night. His stump hurt inside the prosthetic, but instead of flipping back over onto his back, he stayed there, letting the pain ground him. He thought of Pearla. She was uncomfortable at home where circumstances were optimal; he couldn't imagine how she felt now that she was here in this awful place. He could only hope she and Sev had found each other.

A buzzer sounded, and all around him, others started waking up. They were like him…separated from their families, confused, angry at being taken from their homes. He knew intimately just how dangerous desperate men could be.

A soldier came in. He had a rifle slung over his shoulder. His stance was rigid; his face, uncovered now, was impassive.

Someone near Phoenix broke the line, stepping toward the soldier with intent. "I want to know where my wife is," he said, his voice shaky. "Take me to her."

The soldier pointed his gun at him, his eyes hardened steel. One of the other men pulled him back away from the soldier until he once again stood in line by his cot. He looked defeated. He looked afraid.

"Your wife is not my concern," the soldier intoned. "You are my concern."

He turned again to address the assemblage of men. "Form three lines. From there, you will get your work assignments."

The men scattered, milling about on the floor of the warehouse like ants. Phoenix studied them, wondering which line to join. Up ahead, he saw the men from the warehouse…the ones who were talking late at night. They were standing close, sharing furtive glances from the middle line. Phoenix went over to where they stood and fell in behind them.

The men quickly assembled, and the soldier walked down each line. He spotted the man from before, the man who had challenged him, and gave him a cool smile.

"Drainage ditch," the soldier said, cruelly satisfied. "Middle line, you'll work repairing the fence on the south side. Far right, you'll be unloading the supply trucks."

Phoenix studied the others, hoping to glean whatever he could. They, too, seemed as lost as he was. But Phoenix knew the power of being well informed. He would learn as much as he could about these soldiers and this place. That knowledge would help reunite him with his family.

One man from the warehouse observed him, casting him a cautious, curious glance. Phoenix saw his gaze drop to his mechanical arm. The man's mouth quirked in a half-smile; then he turned and said something to his companions. Phoenix couldn't make it out.

More soldiers arrived, two for each line, and they marched them to their worksite. Phoenix's stomach grumbled, but he ignored it. There would be no ration bar this morning.

Once outside, he observed the Kedros camp in the light of day. It was raining steadily, had been for a while, and the ashy substrate that made up the surface of the moon had created a grey slurry not quite thick enough to be mud. The air was acrid with the musk of new rain, but it wasn't the humid, green smell of a wet forest. To Phoenix, it smelled of death. Of hardship. It was the cold, granite-wet smell of a tomb.

They marched them through the rain, and Phoenix stayed vigilant for any sign of Sev or Pearla. He knew his girls could handle themselves, but he was worried. He did not trust these soldiers. Phoenix wouldn't rest until they had reunited.

His line passed by squat buildings and smaller tents. Inside the opening of one, he could see what appeared to be a family…a man, a woman, and two small children huddled around a warming lamp. If there were tents available for families, he would get them one. They would be together again, especially with Pearla's condition.

They arrived at the downed fence. The bleak slurry was ankle deep now. He could feel the cool wetness seeping into his boots. Phoenix took his place at the fence. A soldier gave him a shovel, a hammer, and some nails. Behind them was a large spool of wire webbing.

He began removing the old boards from the fence, the rain pouring off his wet hair in rivulets and running down his face. He glanced over, and the man from before was watching him.

The soldier went back into the dry, warm guard station, leaving them alone. Phoenix worked in silence. His back already ached from a restless night on the cot, but he pushed it out of his mind.

The man nudged him, and Phoenix met his eyes. He seemed a little younger than Phoenix, with light brown hair and intense eyes. "Say, hand me some of those nails, would you?"

Phoenix did so, offering them with a small smile. They worked for a few more minutes, hammering and banging at the old fence.

"You just get here too?"

Phoenix frowned. He didn't know if he could trust this man, but he also didn't see where it would hurt to talk to him. There was power in friendships and associations.

"I did," he said. "With my family."

The man grunted in commiseration but said nothing else for several moments. "Watch yourself," he whispered. It was so quiet Phoenix scarcely heard it over the rain. "This wasn't a rescue."

His empty stomach roiled with the words, and he put his prosthetic against the fence to steady himself. "What is it, then?" he asked, though he was half afraid of the man's answer.

The man put another nail in a board, grunting. "A relocation," he whispered. "Dobani has fallen."

Phoenix dropped his hammer in the mud and hastily bent to pick it up again. When he stood back up, the man was gone, working on another section of the fence away from him.

The rain came down in a deluge. Thunder and lightning split the dreary sky, blocking out what little sun shone on Kedros. Phoenix was chilled to the bone. He hoped beyond everything that his girls weren't as miserable as he was.

Phoenix reached for the wire mesh to go over the boards he'd laid. He couldn't stop thinking about what the man said. *Dobani has fallen.* The words rang in his mind, foreboding and sinister. It all made sense now. The rough treatment, the abrupt evacuation. If Dobani was overrun, all was lost.

He wiped the rainwater from his face. It smelled of sulfur, of the cloudy atmosphere of Kedros. If the soldiers on Kedros weren't Dobani, they were enemies.

His hand shook on the hammer, and he closed his fist against the tremor. He had to find Pearla and Sev. They needed to stick together now more than ever.

◆ ◆ ◆

The industrial-sized kitchen was rife with steam and the humid smell of cooked food. The various odors mixing wrinkled her nose, caused nausea to cramp her empty stomach. Pearla stood at one of the large steel sinks, washing pots and pans. Her hands were red from the hot water and the coarse soap. Her feet ached.

She and the other women had prepared a broth with what they had. Root vegetables, herbs, and irregular cuts of meat. Pearla didn't recognize the protein, and she didn't ask. It sat simmering in large pots, waiting for the luncheon hour. They had received no breakfast and little water, and she felt faint and weakened from the lack.

A woman stood beside her at the sink. She'd introduced herself as Matilda, and her sunny disposition was a stark contrast to their terrifying predicament. Matilda held a steam nozzle that hung down from the ceiling. She blasted each dish Pearla washed, drying them instantly with hot air. Outside, the rain poured down. The building was sturdier than the waxed fabric of the tents, but there were still leaks in the ceiling. They'd placed pots beneath them to catch the water, but they overflowed onto the floor.

Pearla had not seen Sev. She was not in the kitchen, nor did she find her this morning upon waking in the tent. They'd sent her on another work detail then. She wished above anything to have her close.

She washed the last pot from their food prep and handed it to Matilda to steam. Matilda whispered her thanks, blew the pot dry, and placed it back with the others.

Pearla's arms shook from exertion. Matilda placed a hand on her shoulder and gave it a gentle squeeze. "You shouldn't be on your feet for so long," she whispered. Then she reached into her pocket.

She withdrew a few slices of raw potato. "Take them," she said. "It will strengthen you and the baby."

Pearla blinked up at her, wide-eyed. "Where did you get those?" she asked her.

Matilda only smiled. "I pilfered the ends when we were slicing vegetables." Her voice was low and her accent musical; her kind eyes sought hers. She nudged her. "Go on before the guards see."

Pearla took the small pieces and popped one into her mouth. The starchy sweetness fortified her, and she closed her eyes.

A female soldier came into the hot kitchen, her nose wrinkled. "Lunch is in a half hour. The commanding officers need to eat."

She unlocked a pantry filled with fresh fruits and vegetables and an icebox packed with succulent cuts of meat. The scent of ripe fruit hit Pearla like a slap. Plump berries, rich greens, and fat cuts of meat. It was everything they hadn't been given. Her stomach twisted.

"You," she said, pointing to Pearla. "Choose someone to help you prepare the officer's meal. And be quick about it."

Pearla eyed Matilda, and the woman nodded. "Her," Pearla said, and the soldier waved her hand. "Get to it, then. Make sure it is flavorful. We work hard and are hungry."

A muscle ticked in Pearla's jaw, but she said nothing. She and Matilda got to work. They had ample ingredients, and the kitchen soon smelled heady with the aroma of delicious food they couldn't eat.

CHAPTER 12

The makeshift infirmary comprised a large, waxed tent and a dozen waiting cots within. Water poured through the holes in the roof, causing sloppy puddles where the patients were. It was cobbled together, destitute, and barely sanitary. But this was her assignment.

Sev questioned the reasoning. She knew nothing of medical care…of healing the sick. She was a person of action. In life-or-death calls, or even soothing scrapes, she always came up short.

She kneeled beside a little girl with a bloodied knee. She'd fallen in the rain, slipping in the dirty slush of this terrible moon, and had a nasty skinned place. The little one was crying—no mother in sight.

"Hey now," she soothed, and sat down beside her. "Want me to clean that up? Make you feel all better?"

The little girl nodded, large, watery eyes doleful. Sev grabbed some antiseptic from a nearby table and some bandages and tape. She could do this, she silently affirmed. This little girl needed her.

The child's slight frame and tangle of curls reminded her of Lorien…the sibling she hadn't met but already loved. Her brother or sister was going to be this big one day. They would need her, too.

She dabbed the little girl's knee with the antiseptic, and the girl jerked at the sting. Sev frowned. She needed to take her mind off it. To help her think of something else.

"What's your name? Mine's Sev."

She gave her a gentle smile, and the little girl answered her in kind. "I'm Mae," the little girl murmured. Then she glanced up at her, new tears springing from her pretty blue eyes. "I want my mommy, Sev. Can you find her for me?"

Sev said nothing. She cleared her throat, mindful of how tight it had become. "I'm looking for my daddy," Sev whispered. "Maybe your mommy and my daddy are together, and they're both looking for us, too."

It soothed Mae. She grinned, her smile full of missing teeth, and Sev patted her shoulder.

"If you sit still for me, I'll make you a present. Hmm? Can you sit really still for me, Mae, while I bandage your knee?"

The little girl nodded, her eyes bright. She was no longer crying.

Sev went to cut the bandage, and her hands slipped. The scissors fell into the mud.

"Drek," she muttered to herself. She gave Mae a reassuring smile. "You sit here while I go get some more scissors." She laid her hand on her arm. "I'll be right back."

She slopped through the mud, muttering to herself and growing angrier with every step. "Drek -forsaken muddy ol' moon," she groused. "Can't wait to get off this rock…put me here expecting me to help people and—"

She pushed aside the curtained door. There was a man there. He had his back turned. He appeared to be taking inventory.

"Hand me a clean pair of scissors, will ya? Mud gets in everything on this bleak ball of sludge."

The man huffed a laugh, then grew still. He slowly turned around, black eyes searching her face. His mouth fell open. The holopad he was holding slipped in his grasp, and Sev moved to catch it.

She gawked at him. It had been months; his hair was longer, more unkempt, but the pale complexion and striking features were the same. Her stomach flipped when she locked eyes with him. Those black eyes were as deep and as kind as she remembered.

"Sev?"

Sev swallowed. Her hands shook, and she balled them into fists at her side to keep them steady. She finally cleared her throat, nodding. "It's me," she said, her cheeks burning. "How—"

He reached out, gently covering her mouth with his hand. She closed her eyes.

"Not here," he said. Then he pressed something into her hand. "Don't forget your scissors."

He blinked up at him, her eyes trying to transmit everything she wanted to say. He removed his hand from her mouth, flexing his fingers before returning them to the holopad.

"I have to go," she whispered, and he nodded. Then Soren smiled. "I know, Sev." He reached out and grabbed her hand, thumbing over the back of it. His hands, calloused from hard work, were rough against her skin. His smile was a little sad.

Sev turned and left, holding the scissors close to her chest. Her heart thundered in her ears, heat rushing to her cheeks. Up ahead, Mae was waiting patiently on the side of the cot, her arms folded.

She looked up, her smile a little crooked. "I waited!" she announced proudly. "Do you have my present?"

Sev huffed a laugh, and it brought her back to reality. "Not yet. I have to make it. Remember?"

Mae nodded, and Sev cut the bandage with the new scissors and carefully covered her wound. After she'd finished, she took a sheet of paper and began folding it into intricate shapes. The little girl watched, transfixed. Out of the corner of her eye, Sev saw a frantic woman rushing through the infirmary tent.

Mae saw it too. "Mommy!" she said as she threw her arms around the woman's neck. "I got a booboo, but this girl fixed it. Her name is Sev." Mae smiled, toothy and proud. "We're friends."

Sev handed her the intricate paper bird she'd folded into shape, just for her. She tapped the tail, and the wings moved. Mae giggled.

The woman turned to Sev and then surprised her by giving her a hug. "Thank you for taking care of my little girl," she told her. They walked away, back out into the rain. Sev watched as the little girl tucked the paper bird under her shirt so it wouldn't get wet.

She started picking up leftover paper and bandages in the treatment area. She straightened, and Soren was watching her, his arms folded. He had a soft smile on his face.

"Nice trick, with the bird," he said. "I always knew you were a healer at heart."

Sev sighed. "I wish that were the case. I'm not good at this." She gave him a rueful smile. "Not like you are, anyway."

His eyes softened. He seemed as if he wanted to say more. Instead, he exhaled. "Didn't look that way to me. Looked like a natural."

She averted her eyes. There was so much she wanted to tell him…so much she wanted to say about the last few months. She finally turned to face him, nearly withering under the weight of his gaze. "How are you here?"

He frowned. "I could ask you the same, Sev. Where are Phoenix and Pearla?"

Her eyes filled with tears. "I wish I knew."

He gave her a quick nod. "Come on. We can talk in the back." Then he paused, seemingly unsure of himself. "That is, if you want to."

She relaxed. It was such a relief to see a familiar face after so long without, and to have it be Soren, at that.

She gave him a soft smile. "I'd like that," she said.

◆ ◆ ◆

Soren led them to a leaky office. There were no guards back here; a few doctors languished in a workroom partitioned by another dusty curtain, drinking stale stim brew to keep going. He settled behind a desk after offering Sev a chair.

He took a moment to look at her. She was as beautiful as he remembered…those marsh-green eyes and light hair shining even in this dreary place. Her skin had not sallowed in the twilight of Kedros. She must've just arrived.

"How did—"

"When did—"

They laughed, a needed bit of levity in the bleak circumstances. Soren pointed at her, still smiling. "You go first."

She leaned forward, restless energy radiating from her. "How did you get here? When I left Ocarro…well, things did not look good for you."

Soren lowered his chin, resting it on his steepled fingers. "Prescott," he finally said. "With some help from the doctor in the prison infirmary. They both advocated for my release, but to no avail." He gave her a sad smile. "But my sentence was commuted, and they moved me here to Kedros to work the remainder of my days." He glanced at her, his dark eyes as deep as space. "I'm not free, Sev. I'm still imprisoned. Only the scenery has changed."

Sev dipped her chin. "Ok," she said. They said nothing for a while, just existing in each other's space. Then she cleared her throat. "I uh…I never forgot about you, Soren. I'm sorry I didn't do more to help you gain your freedom, though."

He held up his hand. "Don't think of it, Sev. There was nothing you could do. And you had a life to get back to." He smiled, somewhat weary. "When did you get here, anyway?"

She closed her eyes. "Only yesterday. They separated us. I have no idea where Pearla is, or my dad." Sev studied him, eyes sharp. "What is this place, Soren? Surely you know something."

Soren furtively checked behind her to make sure no one was listening. They remained alone, and no one was in the hallway. He lowered his voice. "The Dobani you know is gone, Sev. Overrun by another world. It was a takeover. Mostly peaceful, but hostile all the same."

She let the news settle. Her cheeks heated, and her stomach dropped out. "I can't believe it," she murmured. "I can't believe Dobani's gone."

Soren studied her. He could see the grief at play on her face…the flashes of resistance and defiance that made her who she was. He leaned in. "You can't stay here, Sev. You're not safe. Take it from me."

She blinked up at him. "There's nowhere to go," she said pitifully. "There's nothing I can do."

Soren let it sit for a moment before saying more. "That's true for now," he said. "But things change. Circumstances change." He locked eyes with her, appealing to that fiery spirit he knew so well. "Look for your opening."

Sev gave him an affirming nod. Her hand went across the desk, and he held it in his. "It's good to see you," she said. Her eyes filled with tears.

How could he tell her that he'd gone to bed every night recounting the details of her face? How could he say she was the last thing he thought of and the first name he whispered at the start of each day? Like a prayer...a manifestation. And here she was.

"You too," he said instead. The rest was for him to know, and him alone.

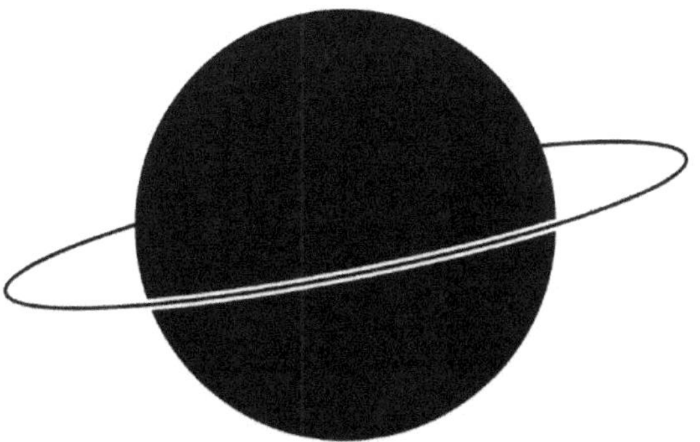

CHAPTER 13

A buzzer rang throughout the camp. It was the luncheon hour, and the men stopped working, straightening with a symphony of groans and grimaces. The rain had stopped, for now. They turned around, Phoenix among them, and eyed the guard station.

Phoenix observed the men he'd worked with throughout the morning. They were dirty and already beaten down by a system none of them understood. He wiped his hand over his mouth. He hoped to see Sev or Pearla at lunch. One man told him that would be his best chance.

The guard came out of the guard station, his uniform dry and pristine, and led Phoenix and the men away without a word. A man pulled even with him. It was the man from before, the man who had told him about Dobani.

He gave him a pointed glance but said nothing. The man's steps grew faster, splashing through the mud with no regard for the mess until he had pulled in front of him.

Phoenix got the unspoken transmitted message. *Follow me.*

◆ ◆ ◆

Soldiers ushered Sev and the other workers in the infirmary, Soren included, into the mess tent without a word. The air was humid; an unpleasant mix of food smells lingered with the musty smell of rain. Immediately, she tried to find her father. Men sat hunched over bowls of stew, dirty and rain-soaked, but none were Phoenix. She didn't see him anywhere.

Soren placed a light hand on her shoulder. "He'll be here. This is the only mess tent in this camp."

She gave a quick nod, swallowing the information but feeling no better because of it. Soren made a face, regret marring his features. "I have to go back. It's not my block to eat yet." He caught her eyes, his soft. "Will you be ok?"

Sev mustered a small smile. "Yeah," she breathed. "I'll see you after lunch."

She got in line. Uniformed workers gave them a tray with a bowl on it. Sev wasn't hungry, despite not having breakfast, but she knew she needed to eat.

She scanned the assembly line of kitchen workers, looking for any sign of Pearla. Women and young girls ladled broth into bowls…tore off chunks of stale bread to soak it in. She found her near the end. There was a kerchief tied around her blue hair. She looked faint, worn out. She had dark circles under her eyes.

"Oh, Pearla," Sev whispered.

She waited patiently, holding her tray. Several times she tried to catch Pearla's eye, but she was too busy. Finally, Pearla noticed her. Sev saw the recognition bloom on her face, saw her eyes water and a smile spread across her face.

Sev watched as a nearby soldier admonished her, and she averted her eyes.

When Sev reached her, she handed her the bowl. "Are you ok?" she whispered.

Pearla ladled broth to the very top of Sev's bowl. She would've given her extra bread if she could, but the soldiers were watching.

"I'm ok, Sev. How is Phoenix?"

Sev frowned. "I haven't seen him. I was hoping you had."

Suddenly, a soldier pushed her forward, spilling half her broth. "You're holding up the line," he snapped.

Sev glared at them with barely restrained contempt. Her hands gripped the sides of her tray. Spilled broth leaked off the sides and onto the floor.

"Sorry," she muttered through gritted teeth, but she was anything but. The soldier watched her with hard eyes until she took a seat at the end of one of the long tables. There were people on all sides, but she had never felt so alone.

She ate the remaining broth in silence. With every bite, her eyes were on the entrance. When he finally walked in, she nearly dropped her spoon.

He was filthy and appeared dead on his feet. Phoenix grabbed a tray and joined the line, trudging in behind the others. She pushed back her bowl, watching him advance.

She saw the exact moment he first laid eyes on Pearla.

His hands clenched on the tray…a muscle in his jaw contracted. Sev could see his entire posture stiffen with anger and relief, both.

They had a brief exchange, and Phoenix approached the tables to sit down.

She stood, risking the wrath of the guards. It was long enough for him to see her, and his smile lit his entire face.

He settled beside Sev, his eyes on his food. Sev could tell he wanted to embrace her, but he was wary of the guards. Finally close to him, she could see the wounds on his left hand…the blood already congealed in the knuckles.

"I'm in the infirmary," she murmured behind her spoon. She was pretending to eat, buying time so she could speak to her father.

He grunted. "I'm repairing the fence," he said between bites. "I'm worried about Pearla."

Sev hummed. "Come by and let me tend your hand. And clean the mud out of your servos."

He smiled, a little crooked, and it reminded her of home. Her chest clenched painfully in remembrance. "Will do, little mouse."

The buzzer sounded, and they parted ways. Phoenix had barely enough time to eat, but he left nothing in his bowl, and Sev was glad. Sev saw him shuffle out with the others, disappearing into the crowd.

◆ ◆ ◆

The kitchen was stale with the scent of cooked food, of stagnant rainwater. Matilda reached out and took a platter of meat from Pearla. "Here honey. Let me carry that for you. You look tired."

Pearla managed a weak smile. Matilda had been so good to her; they had worked on the officer's meal in perfect tandem. It was hot in the kitchen, and the preparation was back-breaking work, but they got it done.

They'd prepared a hearty roast with sauteed vegetables and berry pie for dessert. Pearla had baked a fresh loaf of bread, and it steamed in its checkered cloth where it lay swaddled in a basket on the table.

She gripped the edge of the counter. The kitchen was still stifling, and she had not eaten yet. Her lunchtime was middle block, still twenty minutes away.

Matilda came through the double doors, dusting her hands on her apron. She turned toward Pearla, and her face immediately fell. "Oh, Pearla, come sit down. You don't look so good."

Pearla heard her from far away. Her ears rang, and darkness crowded her vision. She was falling before she could brace herself. The last thing she remembered was Matilda catching her and gently lowering her to the kitchen floor.

◆ ◆ ◆

They brought her in on a stretcher. Her cheeks had high spots of color, but her lips were pale and lifeless. She was still unconscious; she'd fainted in the kitchen and had not yet opened her eyes.

Sev swallowed. *If only I had found her sooner,* Sev couldn't help but think. *I could've helped her.* The regret weighed on her, but she shook it off. She could help her now, and that was enough. It would have to be.

"We need fluids in her," Soren ordered, seamlessly switching into doctor mode. He gave a few more orders to the other doctors there, calling out medical terms and medicines she was unfamiliar with. He turned to Sev, his brows creased in concern. "Wet a clean cloth, Sev. Wipe down her face and cool her off."

Sev sprinted to the supply closet and got several clean rags, a bottle of sterile water. She wet them down and began swabbing Pearla's face. "You're going to be alright, Pearla. Just wake up for me now. I know you're tired, but you have to wake up."

Her eyes fluttered. Soren opened one of her lids and shined a small glow rod in her eyes. He addressed a doctor, his face pinched. "What monitor do we have for the baby?" he asked them. "Ultrasound?"

The older doctor shook his head. "Only heartbeat. It'll have to do."

Soren cursed in Ocarri, then left abruptly. When he returned, he was holding an instrument that resembled a scanner.

Sev observed Pearla's face. The redness in her cheeks was gone. She eyed her racing pulse where it throbbed in her neck. Sev was no medic, but it seemed fast.

She closed her eyes. She sent a silent prayer to Drek for Pearla's recovery. For Lorien's safety. She thought of her father, how panicked he would be if he could see Pearla like this.

As if she had summoned him from the ether, Phoenix entered the tent, cradling his hand. When he saw Pearla, he rushed to her side.

"Sweetheart? Pearl?"

Sev wrapped her arms around her father, comforting herself as much as him. "She's going to be ok, Daddy. She got too hot, is all."

Soren had finished scanning Pearla, and he turned toward Phoenix with his hand out. "Mr. Phoenix," he said with a soft smile. "It's a pleasure to meet you."

Phoenix blinked at him, baffled. "Do I know you?"

Sev laughed. "Sort of, Daddy."

Phoenix took his hand, shaking it absently. "How is Pearla? How is the baby?"

Soren glanced at her where she lay on the cot. "She needs rest. And fluids. The baby is fine. Heartbeat steady."

Phoenix exhaled a breath he didn't realize he was holding. He held Pearla's hand in his mechanical one. His left one was still bleeding.

"Daddy, what did you do?"

His mouth quirked. "Missed the nail. Got my hand instead." He shrugged. "It's fine, dear heart. Pearla is what matters now."

Below them, Pearla stirred. Her eyes fluttered open, and Sev watched as she focused on Phoenix's face, then on hers. Finally, she locked onto Soren, faint recognition lighting her features.

"What—what happened?"

Soren reached for her hand. "They worked you too hard," he whispered. "When's the last time you had anything to eat?"

Pearla blinked, trying to remember. "Yesterday," she breathed.

Soren addressed a fellow doctor. "Tell the kitchen we need broth; we have a patient who can't come to the mess tent. And bread. A large piece."

Sev patted Soren on the arm. She saw her father's face, the confusion at their familiarity. Sev gave him a soft smile. "This is Soren, Daddy. He helped save your life back on Ocarro."

Realization dawned, and Sev registered the light in his eyes. He smiled, lopsided and fond. "As I live and breathe." He offered him his hand, and this time he shook Soren's vigorously. "Thank you, young man. For everything."

Soren dipped his chin. "It's a pleasure, Mr. Phoenix. It's good to finally meet you properly." He eyed his hand. "Now that Pearla's stable, let's have a look at your wound before it gets infected. Sev? Can you flush it with some saline? I'll be there in a moment."

She gave him a firm nod. Sev led Phoenix to another treatment area, and he gave Sev a look. There was a twinkle in his eye, and she dared not decipher the meaning. "So, is that the guy?"

Sev blushed, her cheeks growing hot. "It's just Soren, Daddy. That's all. Now, hold still."

She looked up from her task long enough to see Phoenix's smile.

CHAPTER 14

Once Pearla could stand again and Phoenix's hand was patched up, Soren led them down the hall. There were no doctors in the workroom…no one else around. It was middle block lunch, and everyone was in the mess tent.

He held back the curtain to his office for Sev, Pearla, and Phoenix, and pulled in some extra chairs from the other room. "You can talk in here. Five minutes. Then you should return to your posts, lest someone get suspicious."

Sev settled in a chair opposite her father and regarded him, her eyes warm. "Thank you, Soren."

He gave her a slight nod. "I, uh, better get going. I'm expected at lunch with the others."

With that, Soren disappeared, leaving them alone.

"An army has invaded Dobani," Sev blurted out. Phoenix's face was impassive, but Pearla appeared stricken. She cradled her belly with one hand and pressed the other over her mouth.

"What do you mean 'invaded'?" she asked her. Her wide eyes were rapidly filling with tears.

Phoenix placed a supportive hand on her knee. "Dobani is no more, love," he said, gentling his voice. "It's been overrun. Maybe by these people. I'm not entirely sure."

She gasped but seemed to fortify herself against the news. Her back straightened, and she held her head up, refusing to grieve.

"I knew it," she whispered. "The Dobani I know would never treat its citizens like this. I knew there had to be something wrong."

Sev watched her process the news, admiring her strength and courage. Pearla grew up on Dobani. It was the only home she'd ever known.

Phoenix appeared serious. "What happened today can't happen again, Pearla. We've got to keep you and the baby fed. Between me and Sev, maybe Soren, it shouldn't be that hard."

Sev brightened. "I can sneak her pieces of bread in my empty bowl. She can slip them into her apron pocket, and no one will notice."

Phoenix nodded, pleased. "Good thinking, little mouse. I can do the same."

Tears spilled silently down Pearla's cheeks. "I don't want you two going hungry on my account," she said, her voice tight. "You need your strength, too."

Sev placed a hand on her arm. "We won't be. Everything will be fine, Pearla. It will do until we can be together."

Phoenix considered them, his eyes sharp. "There are family tents," he told them. "I saw them myself. If I knew who to ask…or how to go about the process, we might could get one." He shook his head. "Then at least you two would be where I can look after you."

It warmed her. Phoenix hadn't changed. Still the protector. Still the provider. He was going to be wonderful with the new baby. Sev couldn't wait to see it.

"I'll ask Soren. Maybe he knows. He may be a prisoner, but he has clout as a camp doctor. That has to count for something."

Phoenix dipped his chin. "It's decided." He stood stiffly, not bothering to suppress his groan. "I better head back. The two of you, as well. We don't want to raise suspicion now."

Pearla agreed. "My friend Matilda is covering for me. She's been very kind."

A ghost of warmth touched his face. "Good. Let's make all the alliances we can. It may be what saves us."

They parted ways outside the infirmary. Phoenix hugged Sev, then Pearla. "Stay strong," he whispered to her, and she promised she would.

He was a few steps away when he turned to Sev. "I'm so proud of you, my daughter," he told her. "I'll see you soon." His eyes were resolute, his mouth firm. "We are going to get through this."

She felt the tears sting her eyes, but she blinked them away. "I love you, Daddy," she said as he walked away. "Please be careful." He gave her a little smile over his shoulder, rounded the corner, and was gone. Sev turned and went back inside the infirmary. There was work to do, and it would keep her mind busy until they were together again.

◆ ◆ ◆

Soren made his way back from lunch. He had pocketed half his bread for Sev; she had told him a soldier pushed her and spilled her broth. She must be hungry, he reasoned.

He had resisted the urge to ask her about any injuries…had squashed his desire to run a scanner over her to check for bruises or contusions. Sev wouldn't have welcomed that, but it would've scratched the itch in his brain that screamed at him to keep her from harm.

Soren never thought he'd see her again. He never thought he'd live to see her again. Now that she was here, he was going to do everything in his power to make sure she was safe and as comfortable as possible.

He stepped into the infirmary. It was quiet within. The rain had cleared, and the scant sunlight of Kedros sifted milky and muted through the holes in the tent. Sev was nowhere to be found.

Panic tripped in his chest. Had the soldiers reassigned her? If so, she might be lost to him for good.

His mouth went dry. With heavy steps, he made his way further into the infirmary. It felt like he was missing a piece of himself already.

Just then, Sev rounded the corner, her arms full of gauze. The sun caught on her hair, making it shine spun gold. She regarded him, her eyes up in question. "Back already?"

He rushed to help, taking some of the gauze from her and stacking it in the treatment area. They worked in companionable silence until Sev abruptly cleared her throat.

"I, uh, I wanted to thank you. For letting us use your office. It really helped to get it all out. To just be together."

He demurred. "It's the least I could do, Sev. That reminds me." He dug into his pocket and withdrew the chunk of bread from lunch. "I brought this back. I thought you might be hungry."

Her eyes lit, and she took it with grateful hands. "Thanks," she said shyly. "Dad and I are going to start stockpiling food for Pearla. This will help."

Soren closed his hands over hers where she held the portion of bread. "No, Sev. This is for you. I want you to eat it. To keep your body strong and your mind sharp. You need it as much as Pearla. Maybe more."

She swallowed, licking her lips.

"Promise me you'll eat it," he told her. "I want you to. For me?"

Her mouth twitched. Her jewel-toned eyes sparkled with a curious fire. With a brief nod, she took the bread and stuffed it in her pocket. "Ok," she said. "I promise, Soren."

She'd promised. That was enough…for now. He withdrew his hand. It still tingled where he'd touched her. Absently, he pressed it against his side.

She moved to another box of supplies and began unpacking them. "Daddy said there are family tents. Do you know how we can get one?"

Soren huffed. "It's nearly impossible through proper channels. There's a request system and a long queue."

He watched her face fall. Her hand slowed on the bottles of saline she was stocking. He reached out and nudged her arm. "But I know the housing manager. I treated him for a boil a few weeks ago. He might listen to me if I tell him I have a patient who needs her family." He paused, catching her gaze. "It's worth a shot."

Unexpectedly, Sev wrapped her arms around his neck. It nearly stole his breath, and he hesitated a moment before returning the hug. "Thank you, Soren," she whispered. "I'm glad we found each other again. Even though things are the way they are."

She withdrew almost as quickly, and the contact left him reeling. He could still feel her soft warmth against him, the ghost of her capable arms looped around his neck.

Curiously, his eyes were wet. He blinked hard, swallowing the feeling before it could rise further. "So am I, Sev. So am I."

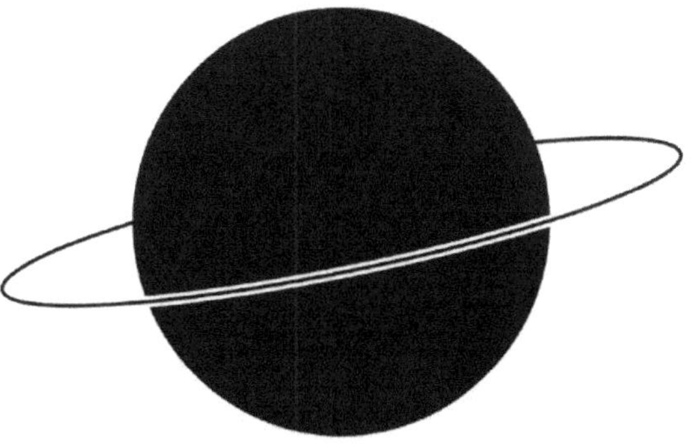

CHAPTER 15

The mud was drying, finally. It lay packed down beneath his feet. His boots had holes in them, and he could feel the damp stickiness in his socks. They'd taken them to the showers that morning, but he was sweating already; the collar of his shirt soaked through.

Kedros was humid—the air dwelling somewhere between a warm shower, which he yearned for, and the steam off a boiling pot. The perpetual twilight glazed the sky in rose gold, not bright but not dim. There was no nighttime…no stars to gaze at.

Phoenix missed Dobani.

The home he and Sev had made there together, and then with Pearla, was gone. The nursery he'd curated with his own hands. Their firepit. The kitchen. Sev's beloved beach. All the things they'd lost…it left him hollowed out sometimes, as he lay awake in the men's tent. There was nowhere to dream of. No home to return to.

The ochre sun of midday cast the world in a sickly hue. He'd spent the last two weeks on this stretch of fence. The work was slow and grueling, but it kept him busy…and kept his mind off the girls.

He turned and noticed the rebel was back. That was a nickname known only to Phoenix; he knew he and his cronies were planning something, but he didn't know what.

The man offered him a small nod of recognition, and Phoenix returned it. They worked in silence long enough for the guard to complete his circuit by their section of the fence.

"Heard you got a family tent," the man muttered. "Must know someone."

Phoenix stiffened. He wouldn't deny it…maybe it would be advantageous to see how this played out, he thought.

"A camp doctor," he said, following it up with a dismissive sniff. "He pulled some strings."

The rebel's eyebrows lifted. "That so. We could use some medical stuff. Could you get supplies?"

Phoenix shrugged, trying to look nonchalant. "Depends. I want in."

The man flushed. He said nothing for a long few seconds. He cast an eye over his shoulder, watchful for the guard.

"Don't know what you mean."

Phoenix chuckled but forged ahead. "Me and my girls. We're included in whatever you're planning. I'll get you what you need from the infirmary. You can use my tent as a meeting place."

The man appeared to consider. Then he held out his hand, and Phoenix shook it firmly.

Phoenix quirked his mouth. "Name's Phoenix," he said.

The other man grew serious, as if he was hesitant to trust him. "Call me Red," he finally said.

They went back to work. Behind them, the guard was getting closer, making his circuit back around. Neither of them spoke again.

◆ ◆ ◆

Later, when the sky had dimmed just enough to show that the day was ending, Pearla tended the fire in their small tent. Sev had scrounged blankets from the infirmary to add to their cots, and she had folded each as neatly as she would've made her bed back home. A single glow rod hung above them, casting muted shadows onto the fabric walls of the tent. Pearla stirred a pan with a few chopped vegetables, scraps from the kitchen that the soldiers ordered her to throw away. Instead, she slipped them into her apron, enough for a meager evening meal.

She took up a wooden spoon laden with vegetables and glistening with fat and gave it to Sev to taste. She waited, her eyes expectant.

Sev hummed, handing her the spoon back clean. "Delicious, Pearla. When Daddy gets here, he will love that."

Pearla blushed, a gentle smile spread across her face. "Wish it were more," she said. "We had a lot of peelings today…not much left on them, though I tried to cut the vegetables pretty rough."

Sev patted her slight shoulder. "It's alright, Pearla. Don't worry. You did good. Thank you so much."

She sighed and took the pan off the flame. Pearla lay back against her cot, a hand over her belly. "How were things at the infirmary today?"

"Good," Sev said. "Soren gave me these to give to you. He wants you to take one a day."

She handed Pearla the little cloth, and Pearla unwrapped it. Inside, there were a handful of brown tablets.

"Supplements," Sev said. "He says you need them for the baby. That they don't feed you enough as it is."

Pearla chuckled. Sev handed her a bottle of water from their little corner of supplies, and she popped one in her mouth. "Soren worries too much."

Sev smiled. "He cares for you, Pearla. We all do."

Pearla gave her a knowing, pensive look. "He cares for you, too."

Heat rose in her cheeks, and Sev averted her eyes. It didn't dissuade Pearla. "You don't see how that boy looks at you."

Sev chuckled softly. "He's a good friend," she said. "That's all."

Pearla smiled knowingly. "Mm hm. If you say so."

The blush was still on her cheeks when Phoenix arrived at the tent. Pearla watched as he dutifully toed off his boots and bent down to kiss her, then Sev, where they sat by the small fire.

He seemed exhausted. The grey dirt of Kedros streaked his hair and spattered his face. The camp let them shower in the morning, but there was no staying clean on this ashy rock.

Sev fetched a basin and washcloth, setting them between them with care. "Sorry it's cold, Daddy. I should've heated it on the fire."

Phoenix laid his mechanical hand on her shoulder and gave it a gentle squeeze. "No worries, mouse. This is just fine."

Pearla withdrew a little cube of soap from under her cot. "I've been saving this," she whispered. "Now is as good a time as any."

Phoenix leaned forward, kissing her gently. Pearla squealed as mud now smudged her face, too, and Sev laughed.

They ate in the firelight, the vegetable scraps and fat filling their otherwise empty stomachs. Pearla felt the quiet gratitude settle in her chest. As meager as her offering was, it was enough for now.

◆ ◆ ◆

Phoenix was in line at the mess tent the next day when Red brushed by him on the way to the table. "Tonight," he whispered. It was all he said the rest of the day.

When twilight darkened the sky as much as it could on Kedros, Red showed up with an assemblage of men. Phoenix met them at the entrance to the tent, a wary look on his face.

"Sev and Pearla stay," he said. "Whatever you have to say to me, you can say to them."

Red swallowed. He cast a furtive glance at the entrance, then considered the men. "Ok," he finally said, and Phoenix pulled back the flap and let them inside.

They settled around the small fire. Pearla served them bits of fried bread, no more than a morsel each, and the men scarfed them down. She gave a rueful smile. "I'm sorry there's not more. Kedros doesn't make hospitality easy."

Red wiped his mouth with a shaky hand and inclined his head in her direction. "Much obliged, ma'am." It was a rare bit of manners from a man he still knew very little about.

He cleared his throat before addressing Phoenix and the others. "We all know why we're here," Red said. "In this tent, anyway."

Phoenix gave a quick nod. Sev, who was listening intently, glanced at Pearla. The other men grunted their affirmations, hesitant to speak.

Red straightened, clearing his throat. "We've got a plan. It's piecemeal, but it might work. It's crazy enough to work."

Phoenix listened. His eyes roved from one man to the next…each of these people played a role, he knew. Red wouldn't have let them in on it if they weren't helping in their own way.

"What can we do?" Phoenix said at last. He eyed Red intently. "Just say the word. If it's in my power, I'll make it happen."

The man regarded Sev and Pearla as if he didn't know if he could fully trust them yet. But Phoenix waited him out.

"We need ether. We're going to knock out the guard at the supply drop. Sneak onto a transport out of here."

Phoenix could tell it shocked Sev, but she had schooled her features into an impassive mask. Phoenix tapped a finger against his knee. "That's going to be tricky," he finally said.

"I can do it," Sev chimed in, and everyone in the tent turned to look at her. "I work in the infirmary. They won't miss one bottle." She tipped her chin, empowered by her ability to help. "I'll give it to my dad, and he can get it to you."

Red looked at Phoenix, then back to Sev. Phoenix smiled. "You heard her. Sev is more than capable. I've put my faith and trust in her a hundred times over with nary a misstep."

Red grunted and turned toward a man to his left. He whispered something to him, and the man gave him a curt nod.

"Ok then," Red said. "You've got yourself a deal."

CHAPTER 16

It was the warm season on Kedros. The surface temperature was dangerously high, hotter than Dobani ever got. Sev could barely breathe. There was an increase in heat exhaustion patients in the infirmary.

She bent over the wound, suture poised. The man had sliced his hand open on a box lid. A freak accident, but a serious one. Soren stood pressed against her shoulder. "Loop this around now, Sev, and pull it tight. That's it. Like you're lacing a pair of shoes."

Sev did as he instructed. The man sat still, to his credit, letting her tend to him. Soren kept his hands off the wound, allowing Sev to administer the bulk of the care.

She entered the last stitch, and she met his eyes. He was obviously pleased.

"Good job," he told her fondly. "You're a natural, just like I thought."

She laughed and wrapped the man's hand. "Keep it clean, which I know is hard here. But do your best." She patted him, and he put his hand on her arm.

"Say, do you have something to eat?" His voice was hushed, as if afraid of being overheard. "Lunch was scarce."

Sev caught Soren's eyes, something unspoken passing between them. An understanding. Soren left for his office, then returned with a wrapped parcel of bread. "Here you go. Just don't tell anyone where you got it."

The man's eyes filled with tears. "Thank you," he whispered. "And I won't."

He left, the bread safely hidden away and a new bandage on his hand.

Sev was cleaning up the treatment area, gathering the bloody gauze and the leftover suture. Soren began helping her without a word.

She was pensive, quiet for a long moment, then caught his eyes. "That's the third day in a row with dwindling supplies. We barely have enough bandages here, and now the food?" She pressed her lips together, concerned.

Soren crossed his arms. "I know, Sev. With the heat and the low mood of the camp. I'm afraid this isn't going to end well."

She stood, considering what he said. It was almost time for middle block lunch, their new slot. He'd got them all moved to one block a while ago. That way, they could all be together. As if reading her mind, he touched her arm lightly.

"I want you to take your meals here at the infirmary from now on. Like you're a patient. If I say you're sick, they won't question it." He looked away as if afraid to continue, then she saw him steady himself. "It's not safe to be around that many people, not with the way things are."

Sev frowned. She pulled her arm away with a huff. "I have to go to the mess tent," she asserted. "I need to check on Pearla. On my dad."

Soren approached her but did not encroach on her space. "Your dad can handle himself," he began. "And Pearla is behind the serving line…not with the general population." *It's only you I'm worried about*, he didn't say.

Her mouth softened, tugging into a bemused sort of smile. "You worry too much," she said half-heartedly. The buzzer sounded, and she dusted her hands on her pants. "Let's go."

Soren relented. He followed behind her, nervous but vigilant.

◆ ◆ ◆

The mess tent was overcrowded, and the air shimmered with a smothering sort of heat. The people there were already arguing amongst themselves, quibbling over a piece of bread.

"Yours is bigger! That's not fair!"

The man with the slightly larger piece of bread clutched it protectively against his chest. When the angry woman reached for it, he shirked away, bumping into someone behind him and spilling their broth.

The man with the spilled broth snarled. He raised his empty tray above his head and cracked the skull of the man with the bread.

People screamed. Sev was a few paces ahead of Soren in line by now. He couldn't get to her. His heart stuttered. Blood roared in his ears, and the surrounding sounds became distant and muffled. He felt sick. He felt powerless.

The man with the bread pushed the woman back, and she fell near Sev. Soren watched, helpless, as Sev kneeled beside the woman to administer aid.

Phoenix was there, trying to hold back the man. He was saying something to Sev, but Soren couldn't make it out. The man with the bread seethed. "Let her alone, girl! She deserves it!"

The man's elbow came down hard, right onto Sev's face. She cried out, crumpled, and fell where she stood.

Phoenix scooped her up in an instant and began pushing his way through the crowd. The entire tent was in chaos now. Men and women scrabbled for the bits of bread and broth that lay spilled on the floor. Pearla, in the serving line, watched in horror as it all unfolded.

Soren pushed a man twice his size out of the way, working his way toward Phoenix. "Come on, Soren," Phoenix uttered in a rush. "Let's get her to the infirmary."

He followed Phoenix as he carried Sev to safety. He was calm on the surface, but inside, he was an anxious ball of panic. *Please*, he silently begged anyone or anything that would listen, *let her be ok.*

Behind them, the tent shook with the energy of hungry, desperate people reaching their breaking point. Soldiers had arrived, and they were beating back the crowds with batons and spraying them with high-powered hoses. Men and women staggered out of the tent, battered, bloody, and wet. Soren turned away; there was nothing he could do to help them now. Sev was the only thing that mattered.

Phoenix burst into the infirmary tent and lay Sev on a cot there. There was blood pouring from her nose, and she had a dark shadow already circling her eye.

He put a hand on Soren's arm, visibly shaken. "Help her," he told him. "Take care of my little girl. I'm going back for Pearla. I've got to get her out of there."

Soren gave him an affirming nod. He packed her nose with gauze and placed an ice pack there. He sat down on the cot and held Sev in his arms. Gingerly, he brushed the hair back away from her face. She would have a shiner, for sure, but at least that animal hadn't broken her nose. Silently, he vowed that if he ever saw that man again, he would make him pay for hurting her.

Sev stirred. She blinked a few times, her eyes rolling, and Soren snapped his fingers near her ear. "Wake up sleepyhead," he whispered fondly. "Please wake up, Sev."

She finally blinked awake and focused her eyes on his face. "What happened?" Her voice was watery, her gaze unstable.

He frowned, holding her a little tighter. "You took a nasty hit to the face. There was a big fight in the mess tent. It was bad."

Her eyes flew open, and she moved to sit up. He kept her where she was. "Pearla!" she exclaimed and pulled away from him. Soren tutted softly.

"Phoenix has got her," he assured her. "They'll be here shortly. You rest."

She closed her eyes. "Ow," she mumbled, and Soren's mouth twitched. "It hurts."

He stroked her hair. "I know, babe. I'll get you something for the pain. We have some tablets left."

He left her and returned with a few pain pills. She swallowed them with a sip of water, then lay back down on the cot. "We've got to get out of here," she murmured weakly. "We're not going to make it much longer."

Soren looked at her grimly. He knew she was right, but the thought of losing Sev, of being here on this terrible moon again with no one with him, was a sobering thought. He didn't think he could survive it a second time. "I know," he said instead.

Phoenix appeared, guiding Pearla gently through the tent flap, his arm around her shoulders. "She's ok," he assured him in answer to Soren's alarm. "Just a little shaken up. How is Sev?"

Sev raised herself up on her elbows and gave him a wobbly smile. "I'm ok, Daddy. Thanks to you and Soren."

Phoenix sat by her side on the cot and reached for her hand. "I'm calling a meeting with Red. We have to go. It has to be soon."

Suddenly, Pearla cried out. She was clutching her stomach and appeared to be in pain. Soren rushed to her side.

"Pearla, what are you feeling? Talk to me."

She panted, then doubled over in pain. Soren kept her from falling over. "The baby," she murmured. "It's too soon."

Soren laid her down, and Phoenix was by her side in a moment. "Not now, please not now," he whispered, barely audible above Pearla's groan. He pinned Soren with a haunted expression. "What's happening, Soren?"

He ran a scanner over her for a tense few seconds. Pearla groaned beneath him; he could see the pain and fear written on her face.

Finally, the readout chirped. Soren pressed his lips together. "It's stress," he said, relieved. "What we call false labor. It'll pass, but it will probably happen again."

Phoenix bent to kiss Pearla on the head, then looked over at where Sev lay on her cot, watching tensely. He patted Soren on the arm. "Take care of them both, son. I've got something I need to do."

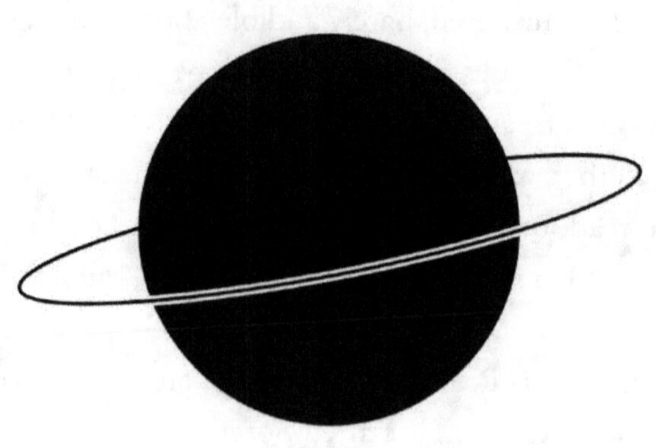

CHAPTER 17

A crack of lightning split the sky, followed by a clap of thunder. The heady scent of a coming storm hung thick in the air. It hadn't rained in a week. The timing couldn't have been worse.

Phoenix rolled onto his back, the only one awake. The fire burned low. Pearla lay beside him on her own cot, as did Sev. They were both tired, he knew. Long days and hard work under strenuous conditions had taken its toll. Sev with a bruised face, her nose swollen and stained a deep blue. Pearla barely hanging on through what had been a difficult pregnancy. The camp was a powder keg about to blow. If Phoenix had anything to say about it, he and his family wouldn't be here when it finally did.

He sat on the side of the cot. Here, in the privacy of their tent, he could sleep without his arm. He reached for it where it stood propped up against the tent and slipped it on, giving the fingers an experimental flex.

After leaving the infirmary yesterday, he'd met with Red. It had to be today, he told him. Red had planned to leave on a shipping transport two weeks from now. Phoenix knew they couldn't wait that long. There was a supply transport arriving tonight. Phoenix would make sure they were on it.

In exchange for the expedited plan, Phoenix volunteered for loading dock detail. Nothing came without a price, he knew. It was risky, but they needed someone on the docks…someone to take out the guard. It might as well be him.

Sev turned on her side, blinking awake. She saw her father sitting there, lost in thought.

"Hey Daddy," she said sleepily. "What's on your mind?"

Phoenix wiped his hand over his face. "Near about everything, little mouse," he said with a sigh.

She sat up, absently straightening her hair. It was down from its usual ponytail, the blonde tresses warmer in the firelight. She finished and leaned forward on her knees. Her face was serious.

"I'll get the ether," she said with conviction. "You don't have to worry, Daddy."

It caused him to smile, and he looked at her warmly. "I never do where you're concerned, Sev. But there are a lot of things that can go wrong besides."

She stood and made her way over to him and settled beside him on the cot. "It won't," she said. "The plan is good." She leaned against him, resting her head on his shoulder. "We're getting out of here."

He nodded, still lost in thought. If it had just been him, he wouldn't be so worried. But it wasn't. Sev and Pearla were depending on him. And Red and the others.

He patted her knee with his mechanical hand. It started to rain, pattering on the roof of the tent like so many drumbeats.

◆ ◆ ◆

Pearla made the bread, working her hands into the dough until her arms cramped. Since the riot, guards were more present. There were soldiers stationed everywhere, even in the kitchen. The trimmings and peelings Pearla usually scrounged were less and less, with rations diminishing. And with soldiers watching her every move, she rarely had a moment to herself.

Then there was Matilda. Sweet Matilda, who had sliced cuts of meat from the officer's pantry and bits of cheese and hidden them inside loaves of bread for Pearla to take back with her. She'd single-handedly saved her from starvation, her and the combined efforts of Phoenix, Sev, and Soren. She owed them her life.

They were standing side by side, as usual, preparing the officers' meal. They'd prepared rich cream soups and grilled meat, along with delicate greens dressed in a spicy sauce. Matilda trimmed the fat off the grilled meat and slid it to her. Pearla could cook with it, use it to add calories to their sparse meals in the tent.

Pearla caught her hand. She gave her a meaningful glance, and Matilda laid down her knife.

Pearla noticed the guards were gone…probably at the table, awaiting their meal. She met her eyes.

"Matilda. If I tell you something, will you promise not to say anything?"

Matilda gave her a reassuring smile. "Of course, honey, what is it? Has something happened?"

She swallowed. She couldn't bear to think of Matilda being left behind, stuck on this grey rock to waste away with no friends or family. Pearla took a deep breath and leaned in close. "We're leaving…tonight," she whispered.

Matilda's eyes grew wide, but she said nothing. Her mouth tugged into a sad smile. "I'm going to miss you, dear Pearla. I truly am."

Pearla worried her lower lip. "Come with us. That's why I'm telling you, so you can come too."

Matilda's grin widened for a moment but quickly dissipated. "I'm needed here, Pearla. Where would the next little mother be if I weren't here to pilfer vegetables for them, hmm?"

Pearla's eyes welled with tears. "You mean you're not coming?"

Matilda shook her head. "You go. Raise that baby in a safe, vibrant place. Dobani will rise soon enough, and then I can go home." She winked. "Maybe I'll see you there."

Pearla gave her a weak smile. She doubted she would ever see Matilda again. "I hope so," she said, her voice filled with tears. "I will never forget your kindness."

Matilda pulled her into a close hug. "Nor will I forget you. Now let's get these men fed so we can eat ourselves. What little it is."

Pearla laughed, wiping a few stray tears that had fallen. "Sounds good."

◆ ◆ ◆

After an uneventful but heavily guarded lunch block, Sev returned to the infirmary early. Soren was still eating; she'd left him ruminating over his bowl of broth and told him she would see him back at the tent.

She headed straight to the back. Soren had given her a key to the medication closet. All she had to do was get the bottle of ether and get it to her father. Easy. Then they were as good as free.

Sev fiddled with the keys, looking for the right one. She tried the third time, and the key slid home. It took one turn of her wrist, and the door swung open.

Sev was rummaging through the closet, lost in thought. She never heard him walk in.

"Sev? What are you looking for?"

She turned around to find Soren standing in the curtained doorway, a confused look on his face.

She was holding the bottle of ether. There was no turning back now.

"Soren," she began nervously. "I can explain."

He looked at the bottle in her hand, then at her. His face fell, stunned by what she held. "Why do you need ether?"

She closed her eyes briefly, then met his imploring gaze. *Get it over quick,* she thought.

"To knock someone out," she said swiftly.

He ambled toward her, his face guarded. "Sev, what are you planning?"

She frowned. "We're leaving tonight."

His face fell. A light in his eyes went out…those dark eyes that held so much kindness, so much tender affection. They were dull with sadness now. With realization.

"You're leaving," he repeated. As if he couldn't believe it.

"Yes," she bit out. She looked up at him with pleading eyes. "Will you help us?"

He swallowed. If he didn't help her, she could get caught, injured, or worse. If he did help her, he would lose her forever.

His eyes grew wet, and his mouth twisted in a deep frown. "I knew Phoenix was planning something…but I didn't know what. Why didn't you tell me?"

Soren appeared hurt, but most of all, betrayed—and she couldn't understand why. "I was afraid," she finally told him, her voice wavering. "I was afraid of what you would think. Of what you would say when I asked you to come with me."

He gasped, like all the air in the room had gone out. His mouth clamped shut. Color rose in his cheeks, spots of blush on his otherwise alabaster complexion.

"Ask me then," he said. His eyes now shone with a curious fire.

Her mouth tugged into a smile. "Will you come with us, Soren?"

He smiled, and something in her chest came loose. "Tell me what you need me to do."

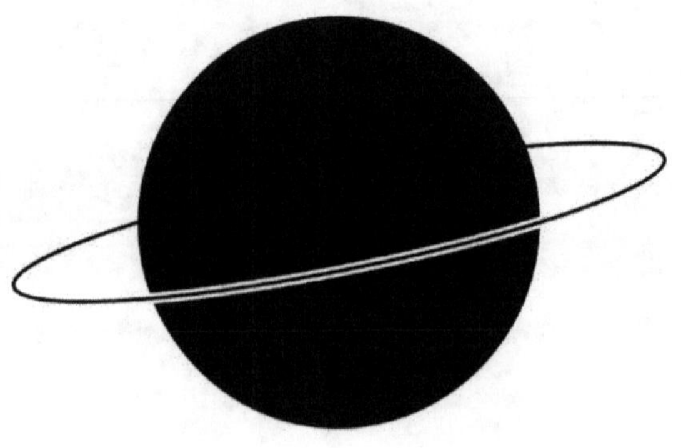

CHAPTER 18

Phoenix and the other men hefted crates in the pouring rain, lightning splitting the sky, their backs bent under the torrent. The bottle of ether burned in his pocket.

Soren held Sev and the rebels in the infirmary under the guise of a vaccination ordinance. It was a natural inclusion for Soren to join them. He was fond of Sev, and she had taken a shine to him, too. Phoenix had eyes. They would board the transport last when Phoenix gave the all-clear. He had an old comm unit on him. No idea where Red had gotten it, and he was afraid to ask. The other one was in the infirmary, turned on and the speaker cranked up.

The bell rang for lunch. Phoenix straightened stiffly and walked in the rain to the mess tent. He would see Pearla for the last time before their escape. He could scarcely wait.

Phoenix waited in line, inching closer to her with each step. He held out his bowl, and her smile warmed him immediately.

"You're soaked," she whispered.

He gave her a little shrug. "You ready?" he mouthed to her, and she dipped her chin, conviction and strength in her eyes. She handed him his portion of bread, fingers brushing the back of his hand.

"Love you," she murmured before the soldiers ushered him away.

Phoenix gritted his teeth. That would be the last time anyone ever kept him from one of his girls. They were getting off this ball of mud. Tonight.

◆ ◆ ◆

Sev checked her chrono. She had not heard from her father. The comm sat solitary and silent on the table in front of her.

"Something's wrong," Red groused. He was pacing in the back room of the infirmary, away from the others there. The infirmary was blessedly empty.

"He should've checked in by now."

Sev eyed him cooly. "It's not time," she asserted. "He'll be in touch soon. The transport probably isn't there yet."

Pearla approached her, a parcel in her hands. "Matilda sent this…it's food for our journey." She gave her a watery smile. "We'll need all the help we can get."

Red snorted. "Best hope Phoenix comes through, or it's all over."

Sev glared at him, her eyes hard. "He'll come through. My father does what he says."

Soren stepped in, breaking the tension. "I'm sure it's just the weather holding things up." He gave Red a reassuring smile. "It will be fine."

Soren had made fresh stim, and the rich, nutty smell of it filled the tent. The others with Red steadily sipped at their cups, but Red waved it off. He was tense already, ready to jump out of his skin. Sev watched him where he stood, restlessly shuffling his feet.

The old comm chirped, then emitted a burst of static, and Sev snatched it up. "Daddy? You there?"

There was a growl from the speaker, then a moment of quiet. Sev listened as her father breathed into the comm. He sounded winded. "It's time," he finally managed.

Red jumped into action. They gathered near the back exit of the tent. Red took the lead; Soren led Pearla and Sev near the back.

They stepped out into the deluge. Rain drenched her instantly, a chill sinking into her bones. Soren squeezed her arm in reassurance, and she sought peace in the calm lines of his face.

He seemed so unflustered. Her heart hammered in her chest. She envied that sort of cool under pressure.

Red hurried them along the outskirts of the camp. The rain was a blessing; no one expected them away from the worksite. The only foot traffic in this area was to and from lunch, and that hour had passed. It was the end of the day. Time for weary workers to retire to their cots.

Or time to escape, Sev thought coolly. The thrill of it breathed boldness into her steps, clearing out the last of her fear.

She glanced at Pearla, at the soft mound protruding from the top of her dress. She had stuffed the food parcel beneath the fabric to keep it dry. Her wet hair stuck to her face. She looked miserable. Sev would see her cozy and warm for these last few weeks of her pregnancy.

Suddenly, Red stopped and motioned to the others. He crouched behind some crates; they were close to the loading dock now. Sev could feel Soren hovering behind them, making sure they stayed hidden from view.

Red stepped away from the group, waving them forward. "It's clear!" he yelled above the din. Soren rushed them forward. Sev tried to hail her father on the comm, but to no avail.

There was a body on the dock. It was the man her father had incapacitated.

She swallowed. *He's only asleep,* she told herself. She'd doctored the cloth with ether herself. He'd be awake before they lifted off. Totally safe.

The rebels led the way, while Red stood watch. He held an air gun at the ready; Sev wondered wildly where he'd gotten it.

Up ahead, through the open hatch, Sev could see her father within; he was holding his hand out, motioning them on.

Suddenly, the shipping transport shook, and the hatch ramp lost purchase on the slick surface of Kedros. The earsplitting screech of metal on metal caused Sev to cover her ears. Ahead, Phoenix seemed alarmed…the transport was taking off sooner than expected.

"Now!" Phoenix screamed, waving wildly, and Sev bolted forward, taking Pearla with her. Soren followed, a supportive hand against her back.

A rebel slipped in the mud, and Soren stayed behind to help. Sev whirled around, horror on her face. The engine's repulsors engaged, their soft whine punching through the sound of the storm. The transport lifted a few feet off the surface. They would have to jump.

"Soren!" she yelled, but he was several feet away. Behind him, Red came barreling toward the hatch, firing the air gun behind him. There were soldiers approaching. The ozone of charged weapons filled the air with acrid smoke. All but two of the rebels were aboard the transport now. Soren caught up with them and pushed Pearla up the ramp, then boosted Sev the few feet it took for her to grab the edge. He scrambled aboard just before the hatch started closing.

Bullets whizzed by their heads, pinging off the stark metal walls. Sev trembled, holding Pearla just inside the hatch. Phoenix surveyed the group, doing a headcount. He paled. "Where's Red?"

Soren looked, and Red was limping toward the half-closed hatch, firing behind him. Blood streamed from his right side, rainwater mixing with it and soaking the ground as he advanced. Soren hung over the edge of the transport, giving him his hand.

"Grab it!" he yelled to him. There were more gunshots, this time hitting close. Soren ducked, and Sev called his name. Below, Red grabbed Soren's hand in a slippery grip and scrambled through the hatch.

He lay panting and bleeding on the floor of the transport. The hatch sealed with a definitive hiss. The transport shook and roared; it was an older hulk of a machine, barely safe enough to transport goods to this backwater moon let alone people, but it would do. Sev laid her head against the rattling metal panel behind her and closed her eyes.

Soren wiped the water out of his face, pushing his unruly hair back away from his forehead. "Help stabilize him," he gritted out, and Sev snapped out of her revelry.

She pressed on Red's wound, and he growled, muttering curses under his breath. "He's lost a lot of blood," Soren uttered tightly. He reached inside his shirt and withdrew a compact field kit. Soren must've taken it from the infirmary.

"Just in case," he quipped, and Sev smiled. The other rebels sat shell-shocked from their near-capture and narrow escape. Pearla rubbed her hands over her belly under the watchful eyes of Phoenix. He crawled over to her and embraced her, whispering soothing words in her ear.

Red was bleeding out; it was gushing between her fingers where they pressed against his wound. Soren flipped him over, spying an exit wound. "Through and through, at least," he said tightly. He glanced at Sev, his tense gaze saying the rest.

It was bad.

Sev threaded the catgut. She remembered, in a horrible flash, stitching up her father on the skiff, how gravely ill he'd been, spore-sick and bleeding. But he'd made it. With a steady hand, she put the needle to flesh and got to work.

◆ ◆ ◆

It must've been an hour, maybe two. They were in the Black barreling to some unknown depot, one that hopefully had a Terminal. Phoenix had not thought of where they would go from there. He hadn't thought as far as their success. For now, he was content to just be, shaky and exhausted as he was.

Red sat half-reclining against the rattle-trap walls of the ship. Most of them had dried off by now, their clothes still a little damp from the downpour and the sweat of exertion. Pearla pulled out the parcel from Matilda and spread it between them. "Eat," she told everyone. "We need our strength."

The rebels eyed the humble offering hungrily. Dried fruits, bits of cheese, dehydrated meat and bread. Everyone took a small portion. No one said a word.

Phoenix exhaled. He looked at his daughter, at Pearla. He glanced at Soren and gave him an affirming nod. The boy had done his part and earned his place.

Kedros was already fading, a dark blip in their shared history. With every rumbling mile they traversed, they were leaving it in the past.

CHAPTER 19

They slept off and on. They shivered, still drying off from the soaking Train of Kedros. Turbulence and solar storms jolted the ship, rattling their teeth and causing them to cling to each other for some sort of stability. The transport lacked the creature comforts that would've made it a safe and reasonable means of human transportation, but it was what they had. The plan had worked.

After what seemed like ages, the shipping transport docked at a Terminal, though Phoenix did not know where. It shuddered, the dull thud of the docking procedure echoing through the hollow ship. He hoped for an automated Terminal, no one to witness their unauthorized exit or to ask pesky questions that could get them detained, or worse. The hatch opened, and the stale, warm air of the Terminal rushed into the cargo hold.

A young man stood there, holding a holopad. *Not automated, then.* His eyes widened when he saw the stowaways, but to his credit, he said nothing. Phoenix sought his gaze, his heart in his throat. He slowly raised his hands to show they were no threat to him.

The man turned away, feigning indifference, and Phoenix sagged in relief.

One by one, they made their way down the ramp into the Terminal. They were stiff from the cramped space, exhausted and hungry. Red, as injured as he was, kept a bloodied hand on his air gun and the other against his wound. Soren led him down the ramp, one arm around his shoulders.

The Terminal was skeletal compared to Central City's—tiny, dim, and nearly forgotten. No crowds rushing to make a connector. No one waiting on a transport at all. It was dark within, industrial. No viewpanes. Low-tech, compared to the larger Terminals he'd been in. He looked over at Sev, who was standing with Pearla, and he could tell she was thinking it through, her eyes wide. This place was as inhospitable as the Black.

◆ ◆ ◆

Pearla paused for a moment, winded from climbing through the hatch and making their way down the endless hallway. The Terminal's walls stood streaked with rust from years without maintenance. There were only a few of these hybrid systems on Dobani, but they were well-maintained, more advanced. This one was little more than a steel skeleton floating in space, the intermittent creaks and groans of shipping transports docking and taking off punctuating the air.

At the thought of Dobani, her eyes watered. She blinked, clearing her vision, and placed a hand over her stomach. She would tell her baby about Dobani, about the quiet beauty and the gentle people of her home world.

Beside her, Sev touched her arm. "Are you ok, Pearla? Do you need to stop?"

She shook her head. "Fine, Sev," she told her quickly. "Let's catch up with Phoenix and the others."

She pulled alongside Phoenix and caught his hand. He turned to her, his eyes tired but full of affection.

"What do we do from here, Phoenix? This place wasn't meant for visitors."

He made a little sound of agreement and brought her hand up to press to his lips. "We'll figure it out, Pearl," he murmured against her skin. "Let me talk to the others."

◆ ◆ ◆

Phoenix observed the Terminal. It was a ghost town, no sign of life besides that technician who'd met them at the hatch. Rickety machinery jutted from the walls…old world technology from an age ago. This Terminal's only human occupant so far had made a hasty exit, and Phoenix was glad.

This Terminal was a shipping depot only, not meant for travelers. They'd have to sneak aboard another shipping barge to make it to wherever they were going.

Up ahead, there was an opening. It seemed as good a place to stop as any. Soren led Red to recline against the wall, then the man waved him off. No people meant no chairs, nowhere to sit and rest. The rebels gathered around him. Phoenix and Soren naturally gravitated toward Pearla and Sev, who stood nearby.

Sev blinked up at Soren, then glanced behind him, just over his shoulder. "How's Red?"

His shoulders lifted in a half-shrug. "Stable, thanks to you."

She smiled. "Thanks to us."

Phoenix grabbed her shoulder and squeezed. "You did good, little mouse." He favored Soren with a warm smile. "You both did."

Behind him, Red had sauntered up to them, followed closely by the rebels. "We need to find a drop board," he said with a grimace. "Map the transports."

Phoenix nodded. "I'll need to discuss it with my family, our next steps," he said.

Red had a strange look on his face. He averted his eyes. "We uh…we have our own plans," he began guardedly. "Not really looking for company."

Phoenix flushed. Of course, this was where they parted ways. He hadn't really expected to follow the rebels, or for them to follow him, but it was a mild shock all the same.

"We would like to offer him a chance to come along, though," he said, pointing to Soren. "Would be useful having a doctor among us."

Soren raised his eyebrows, visibly shocked. Phoenix watched Sev. She had an inscrutable expression on her face.

"That's Soren's decision, of course," Phoenix said stiltedly. "You can talk to hi—"

"No," Soren said flatly, stepping up to where Red stood. His face was resolute, his eyes keen. "I appreciate it, but my place is with them."

Soren locked eyes with Sev, and an unspoken emotion passed between them. Sev gave him a hint of a smile, relief flooding her features.

Red inclined his head as if he understood. He clapped Phoenix on the shoulder, and he and the rebels were gone, deeper into the Terminal to find their drop.

Phoenix watched them go, then looked back at his little group. Pearla seemed tired, dead on her feet. Sev and Soren, a little better off, but not by much. They all needed showers and a hot meal, but that was still a long way off. It was just them now.

♦ ♦ ♦

Sev and Soren followed behind Phoenix and Pearla. Her father was looking for a drop board…a place for Pearla to rest. They trudged along in comfortable silence, their footfalls echoing against the metal floors.

"Thank you," Sev told him. "For staying. Pearla is going to need you for the birth."

He gave a small nod. "You don't have to thank me, Sev," he told her, his voice soft. "I stayed because I wanted to."

Warmth bloomed in her chest. She fought the color rising in her cheeks, but to no avail. She cleared her throat, trying to recover, and met his eyes again. "You're a free man, now. You can go anywhere you like."

He met her eyes, his dark gaze gentle and reflecting what little light there was in the Terminal. "I'll go where you go," he said softly. "If that's good with you."

She laughed, her cheeks red. There was a fluttering beneath her ribs. "Yeah," she whispered. "It's good."

There was a drop board ahead. Her father spotted it around the same time she did. The rebels, having gone off in the opposite direction, were nowhere to be found.

Sev studied the drops, the scheduled arrivals and departures. An offsite switchboard ran the automated system; the Terminal computers received itineraries analog-style. The system names might as well have been written in a foreign tongue; there were clusters and coordinates she'd never heard of.

"Dad, what do you think?"

Phoenix stood at the board, his mechanical hand resting thoughtfully on his chin. He appeared very far away.

"Don't know," he said, though it was noncommittal. He pivoted to Soren. "Take the girls somewhere they can rest," but Sev stepped between them, her arms stiff at her sides, her brow furrowed.

"No, Dad. I get a say in this too. I should know where we're going."

Phoenix frowned, then wiped his hand over his face. "Of course, little mouse. Of course. I'm sorry, sweetheart."

She softened, inclining her head. "It's ok. I'll take Pearla to rest but talk to me about what you find."

He nodded, but his gaze was distant. Sev couldn't shake the idea that he'd seen something on that board he didn't like.

CHAPTER 20

Water dripped from somewhere close by, the drops splatting on the metal floor of the Terminal in rhythmic succession. The systems served by the Terminal were all remote outposts…automated, industrial. A few of them he didn't know.

Then there was Venya. Remote. Rural. The only option, if not exactly ideal.

He sighed heavily, feeling a little of the tension leaving his body. It had been years. Maybe it would be ok.

Phoenix approached the opening at the end of the hallway. Soren, Pearla and Sev had settled on the floor there. One viewport in the high ceiling above them cast a beam of milky starlight onto the small assembly, illuminating the floor. Pearla had Matilda's parcel open between them. A few strips of dried meat and fruit lay on the red cloth.

They heard him coming, and Pearla regarded him with a small smile. "This is the last of it," she said tightly.

He nodded. "We'll give thanks and enjoy it, then."

Sev perked up. "Did you figure out anything from the drop board, Daddy? I never heard of most of those places."

"Neither have I, little mouse. But I think I figured out a plan."

Soren slid closer to Sev and Pearla, attention focused on where Phoenix stood in the pale light from the viewport. The anticipation was heavy in the air.

"We're nearby Venya. It's an old world…out of touch with many of the advancements we're used to. But we can farm the land, make a home there for a while. It will be a safe place for Lorien to be born, too."

Pearla exhaled, something akin to a sigh of relief, and Sev rubbed her back in reassurance.

"If we agree, we can rest here tonight and leave in the morning," Phoenix said. He looked away, his thoughts still occupied.

Sev spoke first. "It sounds like it's our only option. Soren, do you know any of these systems?"

He shook his head. "Venya sounds better than most. Pearla needs to be comfortable and safe these last few weeks."

Phoenix nodded. Pearla met his eyes from where she sat propped up against the wall. "I think we should go," she said. "Sev?"

"I agree," Sev said. She eyed Soren, and he nodded.

Phoenix rubbed his hands together. "It's settled then. We go to Venya tomorrow."

Sev smiled, satisfied they were all in agreement. Pearla motioned for Phoenix to sit, and he lowered beside her. She divided the food. A peaceful quiet descended on them.

◆ ◆ ◆

After eating, they stretched out to rest. Phoenix was curled into Pearla's side, his arm over her round belly. They were both asleep. Sev lay near Soren, but not close enough to touch. She lay awake, staring at the lazy dance of dust motes in the single shaft of light. The old Terminal was full of noise, cracking and popping as it settled.

"What are you thinking?" Soren asked her. She rolled over on her side to face him. He'd been watching her in profile.

"My father's not telling us something," she whispered. "I know him better than anyone; I know when he's withholding."

Soren frowned. "Would you like me to talk to him?"

She shook her head. "It's no use. He'll only talk when he's ready. But I haven't seen him like this in a very long time. It concerns me."

Soren reached out, touching her arm lightly where it lay against the floor. "Maybe you should try to get some sleep," he said.

Sev smiled. "I could say the same." She shivered, a sudden tremor rippling through her. Soren sat up and removed his jacket, draping it over her.

"You don't have to do that," she argued sleepily.

Soren just shook his head. "I'm used to the cold, Sev. Remember? It doesn't bother me."

She closed her eyes. Soren was still awake; she could tell. She could feel the weight of his gaze, the warmth from his body shimmering in the space between them.

She flipped onto her back. The floor was cold beneath her, but his jacket was warm and smelled familiar. She could feel the edges of sleep closing in on her, could hear her father's light snore to her left. She wasn't comfortable, but she felt safe for the first time in a long time.

Maybe Venya could be a new start, she thought, a soft place to land after all they'd been through.

◆ ◆ ◆

Pearla was up before everyone else. She packed up their meager belongings, the canteens that were nearly empty now, and hoped the next Terminal would be better equipped for travelers. Sev and Soren were still asleep, but Phoenix was just stirring.

He propped himself up on one arm, blinking groggily. "You're up, Pearl. How do you feel?"

She stretched, one hand on her back. "Better, hon. Ready to get moving. When does the transport arrive?"

He checked his chrono. "Half hour. Should've woke me up."

She shook her head. "No need. That's plenty of time."

Phoenix groaned, flipping over on his knees and working his way to standing. "These bones are too old to be sleeping on the floor now."

She laughed, soft and light. "Try doing that as big as I am. I'm sore this morning."

Phoenix had finally stood and walked up behind her. He pressed his lips to her cheek. "But as beautiful as ever," he told her. Pearla blushed, canting her head to him. Behind them, Sev and Soren were just waking up.

"Morning," Sev intoned. "When do we head out?"

Phoenix turned to her. "Half hour, little mouse. Pearla has us packed up already. Someone's eager for a proper meal and a comfortable bed."

Soren grinned. "Doesn't that sound nice?" he added, and Sev laughed.

After freshening up as best they could, the four of them left their little alcove and began the long walk to their drop point, nearly on the other side of the Terminal.

◆ ◆ ◆

The transport arrived on time, as an automated transport does, day in and day out, without fail. They boarded after the bot systems had loaded the cargo. The human technician from before was nowhere to be found.

Phoenix imagined what a lonely life it must be, spending your days overseeing a metal hull that needed little intervention from you at all.

His mood was low. He'd tried to shake it on the walk to the drop, tried to talk himself into being excited about Venya, but all he felt was trepidation.

They settled in the cargo hold. It was cold within; this ship was smaller, and there was even less room than there had been on the one they took here.

It did not matter. His girls were safe. Soren was safe. A little temporary discomfort was not an issue in the bigger picture. He shouldn't be worried.

But he was. It choked him…the reality of it catching in his throat, threatening to cut off his air. Tears sprang to his eyes, but he blinked them away before anyone could notice.

◆ ◆ ◆

The cold blanket of space surrounded them. Pearla sat against him. She had her head on his shoulder, and she was holding his hand. He gave it a little squeeze, and he felt her smile.

Sev and Soren sat close, talking in low voices. He smiled to himself. The young man was gone for his daughter; that much was clear. He would have to have a talk with him at some point, man to man, about what he expected of him. Phoenix was still unsure if Sev realized how he felt about her. But it would come soon enough. He knew she would eventually reciprocate Soren's affection for her. Phoenix knew his daughter. He could tell when she fancied something or someone. It would come in its own time. Soren didn't seem to be in any rush, and he was glad.

He thought about Venya. It had been years since he'd been there. His family didn't know his history with it yet…a bit unfair, truth be told. He should prepare them for what was coming. He knew that.

Phoenix closed his eyes, decided. He cleared his throat. "I uh…I need to tell you all something. Let you in on a few things, as it were."

Sev and Soren stopped talking, and Phoenix repositioned himself so that he could see her face. He closed his eyes, hesitant to continue.

"I know Venya. Been there before."

Sev raised her eyebrows. "When?"

He smiled. "Long before you were born, mouse."

Sev seemed to notice the haunted look in her father's eyes, but she let him finish. No one said anything. Phoenix could tell by the looks he was getting they knew it had not been a joyful experience.

Pearla glanced at him, her eyes large. She laid a hand on his arm, offering quiet support. "What happened?" she asked.

Phoenix exhaled a breath. "I was born there," he finally said. "Raised there. Venya was my first home."

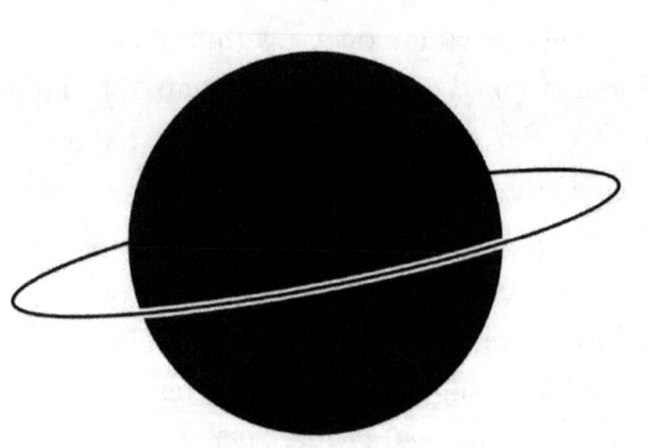

CHAPTER 21

The journey to Venya was uneventful. The freighter they'd stowed away on docked noisily in the docking bay, and they were waiting for the landing sequence to finish. They had rested on the journey, mostly. Phoenix did not elaborate more concerning his experiences on Venya, only that it used to be his home. It only made Sev more curious, more eager to put together the pieces of a father she still hungered to know more about.

It reminded her of being a child, of the curiosity she'd felt when she first met him, after they had formed an uneasy alliance. Her desire to know more about him had burned bright and persistent, but she hadn't pushed. Neither did he. They found a middle ground between knowing and not, and it seemed to work. Had done so for all these years.

The hatch opened, and a puff of steam hissed into the air. The first thing Sev noticed was a glimpse of color, the sound of people. Activity here was so different from where they'd come from.

She helped Pearla stand. Soren reached for her hand, steadying her as they stepped through the hatch. She blushed but did not pull her hand away. His hand was warm against hers, a solid presence in a new and uncertain place.

Phoenix looked at her tenderly. "We made it, little mouse." He sighed, and Pearla came up to slip an arm around his waist. Her father was still pensive and a little more than unsettled.

The Venya Terminal brimmed with people, noise, and varying scents. The air was humid and warm; it felt like summer inside the Terminal. It reminded her of Dobani, and a painful tug pulled just beneath her ribs at the thought. She immediately noticed the pleasant aroma of food. In response, her stomach protested.

"Nutrition station first," Phoenix said. He had Pearla by the hand, but Soren had let go of hers after giving her a shy and somewhat apologetic smile. "We need a hot meal for the journey ahead."

They made their way through the Terminal. People dressed in colorful, loose-fitting garments observed them a little guardedly, but it wasn't unpleasant. The four of them were shabby, she knew—desperate for showers, clean clothes, and sleep.

As they made their way through the Terminal, Sev took it all in. There were vendors selling their wares, food and knickknacks alike. Colorful banners hung from the ceiling, glyphs proclaiming their region of origin. Music played from somewhere. She looked and saw a musician ahead, busking for credits. They'd attracted a small audience.

They arrived at the nutrition station. It was sizeable, with several selections, mostly soups. "Choose something hot," Soren suggested. "It'll warm you up." Sev still wore his jacket, she realized. She moved to shrug out of it, and he stayed her hand. "Eat first, Sev. And keep the jacket."

She dipped her chin, and he regarded her fondly. Pearla and Phoenix were already eating at a small table. They had bowls of thick stew and bite-sized cubes of dehydrated bread. Phoenix put one of the dry cubes into the bowl, and it immediately expanded to a soft and fragrant slice.

When she and Soren had their bowls, they sat opposite him and Pearla. She ate slowly, despite the urge to wolf it down. It'd been days since she had a hot meal.

"Where do we go from here, Daddy?"

Phoenix chewed thoughtfully, his spoon hovering over his bowl. "The village," he said, clearing his throat. "It's a long way…will be a day's journey by railcar. Should get there in the morning."

Questions burned in her throat. *What village?* But she stayed silent, trusting her father to be more forthcoming eventually in his own time.

One thing she and Phoenix had in common was their checkered and unpleasant pasts. She understood how difficult it would be to rehash it, fraught with pain as it was. She wouldn't want anyone pushing her to divulge more than she was comfortable with, and she wasn't going to do that to him, either.

After eating, they settled in to wait on the railcar. There were chairs here, and another nutrition station. Venya Terminal had equipped itself for people, at least.

When the railcar pulled up, Sev stared at it, eyes wide. She'd only ever been on a chute, and that was on Dobani. There were actual rails on the ground, not repulsors. One of many, the railcar seemed to stretch on forever, disappearing into the distance.

They stepped outside the Terminal to make their way to the track, and Sev got her first glimpse of Venya.

It was green, with rolling hills and tuffs of white, fluffy clouds. Wildflowers grew alongside the Terminal, pretty yellow buds that nodded heavily on their stems. She glanced at Soren, and he seemed just as amazed as she was. She didn't know the extent of his off-world experience, but Venya was a long way from Ocarro or Kedros, and for that, she was thankful.

They climbed aboard. The railcar's engine chugged, belching smoke and the sharp stink of petrol, just like the ones in her books. She was used to solar travel, to electric vehicles and the clean-burning fuel of space transports. This was something nostalgic, old but new.

Onboard the railcar, there were plush seats facing each other with little tables between. There weren't many people traveling with them. Phoenix settled them near the back, letting Pearla have the window seat on his side, and sliding in alongside her. Soren did the same for her, and she was eagerly drinking in the landscape like she'd never seen grass before.

Truthfully, between the sands of Dobani and the bleak places she'd traveled with Del, she hadn't seen much of it.

The railcar jerked forward, then dragged along the tracks until it picked up speed, billowing smoke as it did.

Sev glanced at Pearla; she was just as infatuated with the scenery as Sev was. There was a slight smile on her face. She looked better after the meal at the nutrition station and had more color in her face.

Soren appeared contemplative. He occasionally glanced out the window, past Sev's profile, to see the undulating hills, the thick forests of trees so tall you couldn't see their tops.

Her father sat silent, his eyes straight ahead. He looked like the weight of this world had just settled in his lap.

"Daddy—"

He closed his eyes, holding up his hand. "I know, Sev. I know."

She waited him out. Pearla and Soren watched him expectantly. It was now or never.

"I was born on Venya. I told you that much. My mother…" he looked away, through the viewpane. His eyes were wet. "My mother was a good woman. She deserved better than me."

"You don't mean that, Daddy. I'm sure—"

"No, Sev. Just let me finish. It will be easier."

She bit her lip, her eyes large and fixed on him.

"I had a brother, as you know. Lorien." He smiled, looking over at Pearla. "Like our little girl."

Pearla rolled her eyes at that, but said nothing. Her face was fond. She put her hand over her stomach, her eyes tender as she looked at Phoenix. Sev could tell Pearla was just as curious as she was about what her father was about to reveal. She could see her unconsciously bracing for what he said next.

"Lorien died when he was just a young thing. I was tasked with watching him. He drowned in the river." He lowered his head, tears spilling over his lashes. "I couldn't save him."

Sev ached to put her arms around him, but she sat still as stone, afraid of moving lest he stop talking. Pearla shifted, both her hands on her stomach.

When he had composed himself, he sniffed, resolute. "My father left shortly after. My mother was never the same after that."

He took a shuddering breath. Sev looked to her left and Soren was watching him, his eyes soft.

Phoenix was staring at his hands where they lay folded in his lap. "Things were hard. A lot of lean years. I grew up hungry…mad at the world."

Sev swallowed. *Lean and angry*, is how he'd described himself as a young man once. Sev had never forgotten it.

"I did some things that maybe I shouldn't have. Broke some laws. And I left Venya under bad circumstances."

He raised his head, and to Sev, it was like he was bracing for judgment. He would find none from her.

"I uh…I just wanted you to know what we might be walking into," he said carefully. "I'm not sure we'll be too welcome."

He exhaled, and it looked like he was shaking off a heavy burden. Sev leaned forward and placed her hand on his knee. "Whatever it is, we'll face it together, Daddy. You're not alone now. Things are different."

He smiled in that lopsided way of his, and it made him look a little less sad. She and Soren shared a look, and he nodded. "Of course we're here for you, Phoenix," Soren told him. "Like Sev said."

Pearla was holding his arm, and her head lay against his shoulder. She could see the tension in her fingers where they gripped his sleeve, the purposeful pressure. So much strength there, as always.

"There's nothing you could've done that would make me love you any less," Pearla whispered. "You know that, right?"

Phoenix gave a jerky nod, the movement stiff, tears still carving silent paths down his cheeks. Sev looked away, her chest aching. It felt like she was witnessing something sacred…too raw to intrude upon, but too powerful to forget.

Her father had always been so stoic, so conservative with his grief. Whatever happened on Venya must've been bad, she thought.

She glanced down, and Soren was holding her hand. She turned her attention to the viewpane. There was a forest on either side of the railcar, and leaves blotted out the sky. It was darker under the canopy, a false twilight creeping over the hills.

Sev rested her head against the glass, but her thoughts churned too loudly for sleep. Her father's words echoed like footsteps in the dark. They weren't her memories, but she could feel them all the same. Her father's pain had always dwelled just under the surface. She'd never seen it laid bare like this.

Outside, the trees thickened, branches closing in. The land rolled by, lush and dappled with moving shadow, and Sev couldn't help but wonder what waited for them on the other side.

CHAPTER 22

The conductor announced that the next stop would be their last. Phoenix could feel the years peeling away with every mile they traversed…it was like what time travel must be like, he thought to himself. This railcar was taking him to the village in Venya, but it was also taking him into the past.

It was still dark; the sun had not yet peaked over the horizon. Pearla was asleep on his shoulder. Sev and Soren were also sleeping, Sev's head pressed against the cool viewpane, the shadows cast by the moon flitting over her face.

Phoenix closed his eyes, thinking of what lay ahead. He was unsure of their reception; the people of Venya were not what you would call welcoming. And the way he left…well, it complicated things.

He drifted off, letting the railcar rock him into oblivion.

◆ ◆ ◆

The sun was spilling over the green hills of Venya when Sev awoke. Soren was still asleep, his dark hair unkempt and hanging in his eyes. She brushed it back from his forehead, careful not to disturb him. She realized, not for the first time, that she was glad he was here.

Her father was looking out of the viewpane. He had that faraway expression on his face, as if he was seeing something she couldn't.

"We'll be there soon," she murmured. Phoenix said nothing, never taking his eyes off the landscape.

"From what I've seen, Venya is a beautiful place." Sev's efforts to engage him were obvious, but she didn't care. She hated seeing her father so distant.

He smiled, finally looking away. "That it is, little mouse. A beautiful place." He tipped his head to her. "Are you excited? You always did love discovering new places."

She grinned and touched her fingertips to the cool glass. "A little." The landscape had changed…she could feel the railcar slowing down. Squat buildings and a long walkway lay up ahead. The depot, she thought.

He grabbed her hand and gave it a gentle squeeze. "Come on, let's wake the others."

◆ ◆ ◆

They disembarked, stretching in the morning light. They had no bags. No belongings. They had the clothes on their backs and an empty punchcard between them.

Phoenix surveyed the depot, a building that was separated into two parts. A long breezeway joined them, making up the complex. Over to the left, as weathered and stalwart as he remembered, was the general store. He inclined his head in that direction, motioning to the others.

They made their way inside. The few people shopping pivoted their heads to look at them. Old man Potter, the proprietor, was somehow still alive and manning the register. He narrowed his eyes when he saw Phoenix, his weathered skin going pale.

"As I live and breathe," he remarked gruffly. He pointed a gnarled finger at Phoenix, his mouth twisted in a frown. "I'd know that white patch anywhere. What are you doing back here, son?"

Phoenix's face grew hot. He dipped his chin before mustering the courage to look the old man in the eyes. "My family and I hope to stay here for a while. Rest from our travels."

Potter just looked at him, frowning. Phoenix watched as Potter's coolly assessing eyes went to Sev, then Pearla and Soren. He grunted, waving his hand.

"That one's not from these parts," he said, his voice coarse. Phoenix followed his arthritic finger to where it pointed at Soren. The young man just stared at him, unblinking, a sheepish look on his face.

Phoenix stiffened. "He's one of us all the same," he said. "We, uh, we've been traveling a long time. We need some supplies. Thought I would ask about opening a line of credit here, Mr. Potter. I'm good for it, I assure you."

He huffed. "I guess I better let you; you'll rob me blind if I don't."

Pearla gasped. A pall settled over the four of them…shock at the accusation. After a few breaths, Sev stepped forward, her jaw clenched. "How dare you talk to my father that way! My Daddy is a good man. Better than you are, you judgmental old prune!"

Phoenix gently took Sev by the shoulders and led her back to stand with the others. Potter was looking at them in horror, his bushy white eyebrows nearly touching his hairline. "You would do well to keep that ill-mannered daughter of yours in line," he said lowly.

Phoenix bit back a smile, equal parts mortified and proud. She was her father's daughter when it counted. Sev's outburst had been out of line, but she hadn't been wrong. "We'll get what we need and be gone," Phoenix assured him.

They broke away from Potter to make their way down the aisles of the store, basket in hand. Sev glared at Potter, and Phoenix watched as Soren put a reassuring arm around her rigid shoulders, trying to soothe her.

They took their parcels and pressed further into the village commons. Sev was still seething. "What did he mean by that, Daddy? You're no thief."

Phoenix swallowed, patting her back. "It's ok, Sev. We'll talk later, yeah?"

Pearla threaded her fingers through his. "We're going to get through this," she whispered. "I don't want you thinking otherwise, love."

His eyes welled with tears, and he bent to kiss her head. "I won't," he said into her hair. "With someone like you, how can I not?"

She released his hand long enough to wrap her arms around his waist. Up ahead, the canteen in the village commons listed its daily specials on a sandwich board outside. They were all hungry, he knew, and it might be good to talk to a few people about a place to stay.

Phoenix entered the canteen, Pearla at his side and Sev and Soren behind. He scanned the crowd for familiar faces. These citizens were younger, and he breathed a sigh of relief. No more ghosts from his past, for now.

Until he saw him sitting at the bar, nursing a sandwich. He was older, but his dark hair, now streaked with grey, and the stoop of his shoulders were unmistakable. His mother's brother. Uncle Orin.

Orin spotted him before he could leave, the sandwich halfway to his mouth. He dropped it back onto its plate, his face contorted in a scowl.

"You've got a lot of nerve coming back here, Phoenix."

Phoenix gripped Pearla's shoulder, directing her behind him. He made a move to leave, but Orin called after him.

"You gonna answer me, boy?"

Phoenix's mouth twitched. "We don't want trouble. Just looking for a little food. Some information."

Orin pushed his plate away. "You put my sister through trial after trial, but you want a little food," he mocked him. "A little information."

Phoenix looked away. When he met Orin's eyes again, his glittered with tears. "I loved my mother," he said firmly. "No one can say I didn't."

Orin waved his hand. "You're not welcome here." His eyes flicked over the tired faces of Sev and the others. "You or your family."

Phoenix lowered his head, defeated. He moved to leave, and a young woman caught his arm. "He's only here in the mornings," she whispered. "Here. I'll make you some sandwiches if you wait outside, yeah?"

He thanked her profusely and led his family out onto the porch of the canteen. Phoenix scrubbed a hand over his face, trying not to cry.

He looked at Sev and Soren, and then at Pearla. They were all worn down, sadness carved into their faces. His hand shook where it lay against his face. Soren must've noticed how upset he was, because he clapped him on the shoulder.

"We're with you, Phoenix," he told him, and Phoenix gave him a watery smile.

After a few minutes, the young woman from before came out onto the porch, a basket in her hand.

"Here you go," she said with a smile. "I'm Renna. Orin is just an old grouch. I'm sorry for what he said to you." She patted his arm. "You are all welcome here any time."

Something in him cracked then, a wall he hadn't realized was still holding. He blinked quickly, swallowing the lump in his throat.

"Thank you," he managed. "Truly. Say, do you know anything about lodging? We don't have anywhere to go, and we're so tired. Pearla, especially, needs to rest."

Renna smiled. "I've got just the thing if you don't mind a fixer upper. My family owns a small farmhouse on the outskirts of the village. Been trying to sell it. It needs some work, but it'll keep you warm and sheltered. You can stay there as long as you like."

He brightened, feeling hopeful for the first time since they'd arrived on Venya. "That sounds just fine," he replied.

She gave them directions, and the four of them set out on foot. After they'd walked the dusty path out of the village, and the flat plane of the commons had unfurled into rolling hills dotted with wildflowers, the farmhouse finally came into view.

It was a large, two-story wooden structure with a winding wraparound porch. Faded boards with white, chipped paint covered the structure. The porch had fallen through on the last step, and Phoenix had to lead them around the hole there to keep them from falling in.

They entered the dark house, dust flying at the intrusion. Sev fanned her hand in front of her face, coughing. Pearla looked on with wide eyes. She flipped the light switch, and sconces illuminated the peeling wallpaper.

Sheets covered the furniture. Cobwebs filled the corners, stretching across the corners from one wall to the other. Soren peeled back the sheet on the couch, disturbing dust and dead bugs.

"Gross," Sev said with a frown.

Pearla found the kitchen. Green floral wallpaper hung limply from the walls, and grime coated the appliances. She clicked the knob on the gas range and the flame lit. Pearla made a small, satisfied sound and turned to the others. "Kitchen looks good," she called out. "All things considered."

Phoenix stood in the middle of the living room, his hands on his hips. The fireplace was cold and dark, but there were no ashes within. He'd spied a small stack of firewood on the porch. It would do to get them through the night.

"It'll work," he said, dusting his hands. Sev and Soren were already cleaning, using the drop cloths covering the furniture to dust the harder surfaces.

Phoenix stepped out onto the porch, looking out over the yard. There was a flat plot of land covered in green grass. He would break it up, he thought. Plant crops. They'd have a harvest by summer.

His mouth twitched into a smile. Behind him, lights were blinking on in the old farmhouse, filling the windows with warm light like lungs fill with breath.

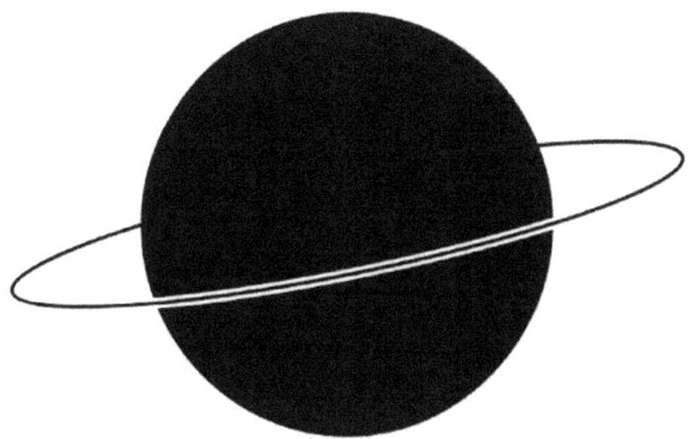

CHAPTER 23

The first thing she heard was the birds, loud and persistent, calling for their breakfast. There must've been a nest nearby…those chirps, as loud as they were, sounded fragile. Hungry.

Sev stretched under the covers. The first thing she'd done last night, even before eating or changing her bed linens, was take a shower. She had scrubbed her skin till it glowed pink; the old farmhouse had hot water, and she'd stayed under the torrent until it ran cold.

The first thing she thought of was how thankful she was to be here. Even if some people were nasty, they seemed safe. No one bothered them outside of the village. There was a solid roof over her head for the first time since leaving home.

At the thought of Dobani—their old home, their old life—her eyes stung. They'd lost so much, she thought to herself. Then she remembered Soren. They'd gained so much, too.

She swung her legs over the bed, bare feet hitting the cold wooden floor. They'd each picked up a change of clothes yesterday, simple slacks and tunics in the local style. Sev dressed quickly and ducked into the bathroom to splash her face with cold water. She blotted her face with a towel, feeling more awake than before.

Making her way downstairs to the kitchen, she noticed Soren was already there.

Sev sniffed, her eyes widening. "Is that stim brew?"

Soren smiled and lifted his cup. "I splurged on it yesterday. Seemed like a necessity."

She laughed. "Indeed, it is. Daddy will be happy." She walked to the pot and poured herself a cup. Pearla had done wonders on the kitchen. The stovetop gleamed in the soft morning light.

She sipped her brew and went over to where Soren sat at the kitchen table. After a good scrubbing, the tabletop had revealed itself to be green speckled Formica, scarred but functional.

Sev glanced up, and Soren was watching her. "How'd you sleep?" he finally asked her, caught out.

The sun was in her eyes, but it felt welcome on her face. "Good," she finally said. "Finally got warm after I found some old quilts in the closet. How about you?"

He huffed a soft laugh. "Like a stone. I was exhausted."

"Mmm," she said between sips. She could feel the stim brew seeping into her bloodstream, waking her up by degrees.

"Daddy and Pearla are still asleep, huh?"

Soren shook his head, his slightly shaggy hair moving with the motion. "Your dad was up before I was, checking out that hole in the porch. I think he's getting a shower."

Sev smirked. "He missed the hot water like I did if he's taking another one," she said behind her cup. She set it down, eyeing him. "What's the plan for the day?"

Soren ran a hand through his hair. It was a quirk that reminded her of Phoenix.

"I'm going into the village. I need to work. Don't have much in the way of skills, but we'll see. Thought I would check the clinic first." He shrugged. "You never know until you ask."

She pursed her lips. "Then I'm going too. Everyone needs to do their part. Me included."

He looked contemplative. "When we get back, I need to help your father. He told me he's working around here today."

Sev's eyes flitted to her hands, to the surface of the scarred Formica. "He's avoiding the village commons," she said matter-of-factly. "I wish he wouldn't."

Soren put a hand on her arm, and she looked up at him. "You saw how it was yesterday," he murmured. "Maybe it's for the best."

She nodded. "For now, maybe," she agreed.

Soren reached for her empty cup and put them both in the sink. "Let's make them breakfast," he said. "We picked up a few eggs yesterday, some salt meat." He looked around and began opening cabinets. "There's a skillet around her somewhere," he mused. "No farmhouse is complete without it."

He finally found what he was looking for and held it up with a smile. His grin was wide, black eyes sparkling.

Sev smiled. "Let's do it," she said, getting up to help.

◆ ◆ ◆

When Pearla and Phoenix emerged from the bedroom, the kitchen smelled richly of cured meat and grease. His stomach rumbled.

"What's this?" he asked good-naturedly. He was still without his arm.

Sev flourished a platter of eggs before setting it on the table. "Breakfast Daddy. Pearla, grab a plate. I don't want you to lift a finger. We're gonna clean all this up, too."

Soren finished frying the meat and put it alongside the eggs, transferring it from the skillet to the platter with care. They all sat down, and Phoenix gave thanks. He felt closer to Drek here on Venya, more attuned to his roots. Not all his upbringing had been bad, he thought.

Pearla took a bite and hummed at the taste. "This is delicious you two. Any time you get the urge to cook, you're hired."

Sev laughed, and Soren gave a comical little bow. Phoenix smiled. It was a simple breakfast, but the gesture warmed his heart.

He watched as Sev chewed. She was a little quiet as the meal wore on. There was something on her mind, to be sure.

She finally broke. "Daddy…can I ask you something?"

Phoenix wiped his mouth and set his fork down. "Of course, little mouse. Always."

Her face was troubled. Phoenix suspected why.

"What did that old man mean yesterday that you would steal from him? Why would he say that?"

Phoenix sat back in his chair. The morning light was warm through the window; that, plus the cooking Sev and Soren had done, left the kitchen cozy, bereft of the early chill.

He looked out the window, wondering how to tell her. Pearla reached for his arm.

"You don't have to, hon. If you don't want to."

Sev agreed. "I'm sorry, Daddy. I didn't mean to make you feel bad."

He waved her off. "It's no matter, little mouse. I, uh…" He stopped talking abruptly, gathering himself, and started again. "When I was a boy. Well, a little older than that. I took some things that didn't belong to me. My mother and I were very poor. It's no excuse, but those actions tarnished my reputation in the village. That, and the way Lorien died. Well…let's just say that around here, I'm the last person some of the older folks want to lay eyes on."

When Phoenix finally faced Sev and Pearla, they had tears in their eyes. Soren reached out and lay a hand on his arm. "There's no shame in surviving," he assured him. "Or in providing for your family."

He lowered his head. "It was wrong, though. And I regret it. I feel like it hurt my mother, in the end, and now it's hurting you."

Sev shook her head. "Don't apologize, Daddy." Her eyes still glittered with tears. "I love you, regardless. And I always will."

They finished their breakfast. Phoenix felt lighter…purposeful. The day looked just a little brighter.

Despite their protests, Pearla went into the living room to continue tidying up, citing the need for something to do. Sev and Soren took off for the village. Phoenix walked out onto the porch, the spare boards he'd found in the shed stacked by the hole there.

He got to work with the patch job. When he'd finished a few hours later, he stood and appraised his work. It wasn't perfect, but it was solid. Safe. That's what counted.

Phoenix took the hammer and the rest of the nails back to the shed. There was a large tarp covering something big that he hadn't noticed in his predawn exploration. His curiosity got the best of him, and he pulled it off.

The tarp fell onto the ground with a flurry of dust. A tractor sat beneath, old, but unblemished.

Phoenix couldn't believe his luck. He climbed up top and turned the key. The engine whined but wouldn't turn over.

He got down and popped the hood. Phoenix rolled up his sleeves and got to work. It would be midday soon, the hottest part. The quicker he could get her up and running, the better.

◆ ◆ ◆

Sev and Soren arrived at the canteen just as the lunch crowd was dispersing. He watched Sev take a steadying breath; the treatment they'd received at the hands of the locals had been hard for her.

But no one said anything. Beyond a few curious looks and whispers, they entered the canteen without incident.

Renna came to their table and offered them something to drink. She greeted them with a smile and told them the daily special.

Soren listened politely, letting her finish. "I was actually hoping to visit the clinic," he told her.

A man overheard and scoffed. "Ain't no doctor at the clinic," he said gruffly. "There's not been a doctor for months now. So, there's no use goin'."

Soren shot Sev a pointed look. "Would still like to go, if it's all the same." He smiled amiably. "To see for myself."

The man went back to his food, having lost interest. Renna gave them directions, and, after they had finished their drink, they headed off.

Soren walked quickly, eager to see the clinic. He watched Sev as she eyed the villagers warily. His Sev, he thought. Always full of fire. He wouldn't trade that spark in her for anything.

Up ahead, Soren saw a clapboard building with a crooked sign. The door was ajar, the glass on it cracked. They pushed their way inside.

It was clean within, but in disarray. He appraised some of the equipment; the technology was antiquated, downright nonexistent when compared to Ocarri medicine. There were bandages and a single scanner in plain view. The several beds inside were empty.

"May I help you?"

They whirled around, and a middle-aged woman with light hair stood in the doorway. She was looking at them curiously, her arms folded over her chest.

Soren smiled. "I hope you can. I was told there's not a doctor here. That there hasn't been one for some time. That so?"

She inclined her head. "That's right. I'm the only medic here. Everyone else left when Doc did." She eyed them both. "One of you sick?"

Sev's eyes were warm, and Soren shook his head. "I'm a doctor," he said, holding out his hand for her to shake. "My name is Soren. This is Sev."

The woman grinned, her eyes lighting excitedly. "Well, what can I help you with? You weren't…you weren't thinking of staying, were you?"

Sev laughed. "We just got here, actually, so yes."

The woman offered them a seat in the middle of the clinic. The place was clean. She'd kept it up well, even with no doctor. Crisp white lines covered the beds, and there was no dust anywhere.

"I'm Greta," the woman said. "I treat who I can, but there's a limit to what I can do."

Soren regarded her. "What is the hiring process? Who do I need to speak to?"

Greta smiled. "The board chairperson. He can be by today. I'm sure he'll hire you, Soren."

His mouth twitched upward. "And Sev, too," he said. "She's my assistant. If I'm hired, then so is she."

Greta appeared taken aback by that, but she quickly recovered. "Of course," she finally said. "Can I get you anything?"

Sev shook her head. "We're just going to have a look around, if that's ok."

The woman nodded, then left them in the clinic alone.

Soren turned to Sev, his eyes bright. "I feel good about this, Sev. Think of the people we can help here." He put his hands on her shoulders as if trying to transmit his enthusiasm.

Sev placed a hand on his arm before pulling away, looking around the small clinic. "It has potential," she admitted. "It feels right."

Soren arrived at the back of the clinic and began opening cabinets, taking inventory. They would need a lot just to get this place going again. But it could work, he thought. With Sev, they would make it work.

◆ ◆ ◆

They walked home, taking their time. The chairperson had advanced them their first month's pay, and Sev and Soren had gone straight to the general store to pay their bill, plus make some other purchases. Old Mr. Potter had nothing to say, good or bad, and for Sev, that was enough.

The hills were awash in the orange ribbons of light that marked the end of the day. When the house came into view, the first thing Sev saw was the freshly tilled earth, the field ready for planting. Something bloomed within her, something akin to hope and new beginnings.

They brought their wares inside. Phoenix was sitting on the couch, freshly showered. He had the satisfied exhaustion of a day's work well done written on his face. He held Pearla's feet in his lap. She was knitting.

"Where did you get the yarn?" Sev asked her, and Pearla appeared thoughtful. "Found it in a drawer in the study. Figured I'd make myself useful…knit Lorien a blanket."

Phoenix gripped her feet in his hands, massaging gently. "You're plenty useful, my love." He studied Sev, his eyes fond. "Tell me how the trip to the village went." He hesitated. "Any problems?"

Soren shook his head. "None, Phoenix. And guess who's the new doctor?"

Pearla gasped. "You're kidding," she said, delighted. She lowered the little square of yarn, momentarily forgetting it.

"And I'm his assistant," Sev added, beaming.

Soren and Sev sat on the loveseat facing the fire, close enough to touch, but they did not. The flames licked at the logs, casting golden light over the little room. It felt warm and cozy in a way that whispered of home.

Venya was new, but this feeling of belonging…of family, was something she was wonderfully familiar with.

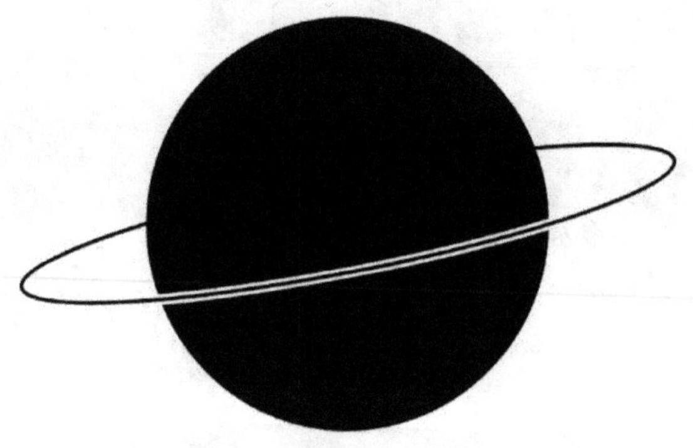

CHAPTER 24

The walk to the village commons was meditative. Sev could feel the energy vibrating off Soren. He was excited but seemed nervous too. It was their first day, so she understood.

She placed a hand on his arm, feeling the tension there. "Relax," she told him. It was early morning. The sun was just pouring over the hills, bright and warm. The air still held the overnight chill, not biting enough for a coat, but cold enough to prickle the skin on her arms.

He gave her a nervous laugh. His eyes were lighter in the sun, deep black gone to brown. "I just want everything to be right," he said. "I want to do well."

She withdrew her hand. "You will," she assured him. "And I'll help you."

He studied her face, his eyes twinkling. "With a medic like you, how can I fail?"

Sev huffed. "I'm just an assistant, Soren. They only hired me because of you."

It looked like it wounded him. He caught her hand, and she glanced at him where he was backlit against the rising sun.

"Never downplay your worth, Sev," he told her. "You're as capable a medic as I've ever seen. Don't forget that."

Her hands tingled where they touched. He abruptly released her, self-consciously drawing his hand close to his body, as if she had burned him.

"I won't," she said. "And whatever we find at the clinic, we'll deal with together."

◆ ◆ ◆

They made it to the village commons just as the day was warming up. There were a few people having their breakfast at tables outside the canteen. Others milled around the fountain in the middle of the village. They all wore the loose-fitting, colorful tunics popular on Venya. Sev and Soren had on something similar.

The clinic lay up ahead, silent and still. Someone had changed the lettering on the door. It now featured Soren's name, and they had replaced the glass.

He smiled, a faint blush tinting his fair skin, and it warmed Sev to see it. If she had her holopad with her, she would've taken a picture.

They pushed inside. The clinic was in order, unlike yesterday. Greta had changed the beds and put away the supplies. She'd dusted the cabinets and exam tables. Everything shone with a gleam of newness, despite the age.

There was no one there.

Soren and Sev peeked into the waiting room just to make sure. It was empty. Light shone through the windows facing the street. Holopads sat on the end tables, waiting to be used for check in. Paper periodicals, like the ones her father favored, sat folded on a shelf alongside various pamphlets and magazines.

Soren turned to find Greta in the doorway, watching them with a hint of a smile. "It's early," she said. "I wouldn't get too disheartened."

He smiled, but it was tight. She and Soren went back into the clinic and sat down in the chairs there to wait for their first patient.

◆ ◆ ◆

Greta made stim brew. The rich aroma filled the empty clinic, cutting through the clean, antiseptic smell. Sev was organizing the supply closet for the second time that morning.

Soren was nursing a glass of water, wondering what he was doing there. "Is it me?"

Sev turned around at the sound of his voice. No one had really said much, and the morning had passed in silence.

She cocked an eyebrow. "What do you mean is it you?"

He sighed. "I mean, because I'm an off-worlder. Because I look different."

She smiled. "Different or not, who wouldn't want to see a handsome doctor like you? I'd be faking symptoms just to get a checkup."

Soren laughed, which he suspected was Sev's goal. He couldn't help the blush that dusted his cheeks. "You're already stuck with me, so there's no need for that."

She sauntered closer to him, within reach of where he sat, her hands on her hips. "Even so," she said, a wry grin on her face.

He accepted the stim brew from Greta. He could tell she felt bad about no one showing up. The village was skeptical of him, he knew. There had to be another way.

Soren sipped the stim brew, thinking. It was approaching the luncheon hour, and his stomach rumbled. He put down his cup and held out his hand.

"Come on, Sev. Let's have a bite. Maybe things will pick up after lunch."

They walked across the village commons to the canteen. There were more people out now. The village was bustling.

They entered and sat at one of the few open tables. Renna gave them menus and asked them about the farmhouse. Sev answered her the most; he still felt distracted and a little down.

The two men at the next table were taking loud enough for him to hear. He pretended to be casual, but Soren eavesdropped while Sev read the menu.

"It's a shame what happened to that little girl. Nothing to be done, though. When a child gets sick like that."

The man across from him took a swig of his drink. "I feel for the parents," he said, his voice grave. "She got sick at school, from what I understand. There are some others showing signs, too."

Soren cleared his throat and looked over at the two men. "What's this about a sickness?" His face reddened, and he quickly apologized. "I didn't mean to overhear, it's just…well, I'm the new doctor in the village. If there's something I can do, I'll do it."

Sev was watching him, he knew. The men shared a look, then one cleared his throat. "The school knows more about it," he said gruffly, obviously unwilling to share more with a stranger.

"Where is the school?" Sev asked. She was listening now, having finished reviewing the menu, and was obviously interested.

The man gave them directions. It was outside the village, almost the route they took to the farmhouse. Soren looked at Sev, and he realized they were both thinking the same thing.

◆ ◆ ◆

The walk to the school was uneventful. Soren's steps were quick, fueled by a renewed purpose. Sev knew how let down he'd been when no one showed up for treatment at the clinic. This fact-finding mission to the school was the right move.

The headmistress met them at the door. She appeared harried, worn-out. "May I help you?"

Soren offered his hand. "My name is Soren. I'm the new doctor here. I heard that some of your students might need treatment. Is that so?"

She gave him a tired smile. "Only all of them. It happened just this morning. They are coughing, running fever. Many of them complain of body aches. I don't know how to help them, honestly, and they can't do their work because they feel so bad."

She motioned them inside. "Come in, won't you? We've tried to keep the children comfortable until their parents arrive."

Sev and Soren followed her inside. The school was neat and clean, well-stocked with books, but lacking the technology one would expect of a learning center based on another world. Her father had said Venya was a little behind the times, and now she could see what he meant.

They settled in the headmistress's office. There were posters with glyphs touting the importance of reading, of math aptitude. Some sunny children were advertising the virtue of doing your homework.

Sev could see Soren running through the possibilities in his quick mind…how best he could help. "Could their parents bring them to the clinic? Or have they already?"

The headmistress shook her head. "The parents are skeptical of seeking treatment since the doctor left the village a few months back. There hasn't been any medical care here for so long. They may not know about you."

Sev brightened. "Could we stay here until the parents arrive? We could introduce ourselves to the parents…maybe gain their trust."

She watched his face, garnering his reaction. She could tell he liked the idea.

The headmistress agreed. Behind her in another room, Sev heard the wheezing, wet sound of children struggling to breathe, the groans of the fevered and suffering. She hoped the parents would come soon, and that they were open to medical intervention.

Little by little, the parents trickled in. The headmistress allowed them to reunite with their children but prevented them from leaving just yet. They were all gathered in the cafeteria, parents with their children hugged tightly to them. Sev could see the fear clearly writ on their faces.

When they had all gathered, Soren stood on a small platform near the front of the room. He cleared his throat. Sev could see his hand tremor slightly, and she silently willed him all the strength she could muster.

"Parents…good people of Venya. My name is Soren. I am your new doctor. Just started today, in fact."

He smoothed his tunic, a nervous habit, just to give him something to do with his hands. "I know you are frightened. I know you want the best for your children. But this illness needs treatment. The children need medicine."

As if to underscore his words, a few children coughed. Others sniffled. Mothers blotted noses and held cold compresses to fevered foreheads.

"Please come by the clinic with your children. I will treat them to the best of my ability." He gestured to Sev, a small smile on his face. "This is Sev. She is a skilled medic and will assist me."

Sev gave the crowd a small wave. She took in the frightened faces of the parents…the fevered blush of the children. She could only hope they were listening to what Soren was saying.

He lowered his head for a moment, as if gathering his strength. "I am not from Venya, as you can tell. I am Ocarri. My home world of Ocarro is known for its advancements in medicine. I trained there for many years before I became a doctor."

When he spoke again, his voice was softer, more pleading. "I know I look different. But on the inside, we are all the same. We all hurt. We all love. And sometimes, we become sick and need treatment."

He stepped down off the platform and looked into the eyes of the Venyan parents. Sev could tell that most of them were listening to every word.

"You can trust me with your children," he finally said. He had his hands out to the side, palms up. "I hope to see you at the clinic soon."

He approached Sev and grabbed her hand. They walked out of the school together. Sev felt lighter, like the meeting had been a success. She could only hope that was true.

◆ ◆ ◆

When they returned to clinic, the waiting room was full.

Where silence had once lingered, the air now buzzed with voices and life. Soren immediately sprang into action, instructing Greta to send the first few children in. Sev got them settled on the exam table. She ran the scanner over them and gave them infusions to help with the fever while Soren listened to their breathing.

"Will she be alright?"

The mother was young; Sev could see the fear on her face. The little girl she'd brought in had pudgy cheeks and a high temperature.

Soren lay his hand on her arm. "She will be now," he said, smiling. "We caught it early."

The young children all had a viral infection Soren had seen before on Ocarri. Something common in children, he had said. They treated patients all afternoon until the sun sank beneath the horizon. Neither of them had supper. When the last parent and child left, Soren sank back against the door and closed his eyes.

"We did it," he said with a tired smile. Greta was tidying up; she'd been instrumental in the thick of it, making cold compresses and fever tonics for Sev to administer. It had truly been a group effort.

Just as they were packing up to leave, the bell over the clinic door rang. Sev turned, and her mouth fell open briefly as she registered who it was.

It was old Mr. Potter.

He came in sheepishly, bent over his cane, and sat down in the waiting room. Soren walked in, and the man gave him a sharp look. "Heard this was where you came when you didn't feel too good."

It made Soren smile, and he waved him back into the exam room. Soren and Sev treated Mr. Potter's aching knee, and the old man left in a lot better mood than when he came in.

Soren picked up the tools on the exam table and put them away. Greta had gone home for the night.

Sev laid a hand on his shoulder, feeling the tension there. "You got the old man stamp of approval," she teased. "Come on," she said. "We've got a long walk back, and it's dark."

He offered her his arm, old-world style, and she giggled. They walked out together into the starry night. Sev was exhausted, but she'd never felt more fulfilled. She knew from the light in his eyes that Soren felt that way, too.

CHAPTER 25

Phoenix leaned into the morning. It was tranquil…the birds called to one another, occasionally dipping above where he worked in the field. There was a gentle wind that dried the sweat on the back of his neck. He had planted three rows; it was sweltering work but rewarding. Dirt caked his hands, and a new callous had formed where he gripped the spade. But Phoenix knew that with every seed he sowed, it would reap a harvest for his family.

And a surprise for Sev. He had planted one row with seeds from Dobani; they'd been in his pocket when they were ushered into the trucks, and he'd kept up with them ever since.

It quirked his mouth. A little taste of home. Something to remember it by.

Phoenix dug into the soft ground, and his spade struck rock. The handle broke, splintering in his hand. One wooden shard stuck through his skin, and he dropped the broken tool, cursing his luck. Drops of blood fell onto the dark soil.

He wiped his hand on his pants. The bleeding had stopped already. There wasn't another spade in the shed, he knew. He'd need to go to the village.

Phoenix hadn't been since the first day they arrived, and he wasn't looking forward to it. Things were working out for Soren and Sev, and he was glad.

He had stayed behind with Pearla, letting the gossip cool and the dust of their abrupt appearance settle.

His back twinged as he stood, and he grimaced. Phoenix was not old, but he wasn't young, either. He'd pushed his creaky bones to the limit these past days.

Phoenix dusted his hands on his pants and went inside to get cleaned up.

♦ ♦ ♦

It was the luncheon hour, and the village commons was swarming with people. Phoenix had talked himself into more confidence than he thought capable, resolute in meeting any opposition he faced with a kind word. These people didn't know him…the elders knew a shadow of who he was, but Phoenix wasn't that man now. Somehow, he would prove himself.

He pushed into the general store, waving to Mr. Potter. The man huffed, then turned to one of his customers sitting at the soda fountain. He gave him a cursory glance, and his stomach lurched.

It was his Uncle Orin.

He said nothing. Phoenix picked up a new spade and carried it to the register. Orin sat only feet away, scowling at him.

He was staring, so Phoenix forced a polite smile. He paid hurriedly and left with the spade tucked under his arm, eager to get back to the farmhouse.

Orin followed him out.

"Cordera was never the same after you left," he said, his voice hard. There were others there sitting on the porch of the general store. Phoenix could feel their eyes on him…cool. Impassive.

He swallowed. "I never meant to hurt her," he said, his voice thick. "I loved my mother very much."

Orin rapped his cane on the porch in frustration. "You loved her into the grave! You and your thieving ways. Law-breaking, good-for-nothing, ne'er-do-well." Orin locked eyes with him. Phoenix felt his own eyes well, could feel the tears coming unbidden.

"You should've never come back here with that ragtag family of yours."

Phoenix cleared his throat. "Think what you want of me, Uncle," Phoenix began. "But don't besmirch my family. They've done nothing wrong."

Orin sniffed. He looked over at the onlookers. There were quite a few now. Some watched Phoenix with something akin to sympathy.

"Yet," he said derisively, then shouldered his way back into the store.

Phoenix hung his head. His grip on the spade faltered, and he readjusted it. He looked at the onlookers, some with pity on their faces. "Sorry for the scene," he said, abashed. "I'll be on my way now."

He felt eyes on him as he made his way across the village commons. His stomach rumbled; he hadn't eaten since breakfast.

Phoenix stopped by the canteen. He leaned his new spade by the door, confident of its safety. A young woman waited on him as soon as he sat down, a broad smile on her face.

"Are you Sev's dad? You are, aren't you?"

He nodded, his eyes warm. Maybe not everyone had made up their mind about him, after all, he thought. "Name's Phoenix."

She grinned. "I'm Renna. I've heard so much about you."

I bet, he thought grimly, but he did not say. He ordered a sandwich, ignoring the whispers, the stares in his direction.

When Renna brought out his meal, he thanked her. He still felt low from his encounter with Orin. If Pearla had been there, she would've called him out on being so quiet.

"Say Renna. Is Cordera's old homestead still standing? Out on the west ridge?"

She thought for a moment. "I think so. Barely, if that. Do you need directions?"

He smiled and shook his head. "No, I know the way."

◆ ◆ ◆

Phoenix diverged at the fork that would take him to the farmhouse. It was instinct, mostly. His steps were slow, calculated. He couldn't help but repeat what Orin had said, turning it over in his mind on an endless loop.

You loved her into the grave.

Venyan funerals didn't involve burials. There was a ceremony…he remembered Lorien's vividly. Then the villagers sent the body out onto the water, that person's last journey into the afterlife.

Phoenix had not been here for his mother's home going. He was long gone by that point. If Orin was right, that she grieved herself to death, then he didn't deserve any good thing that had ever happened to him. He didn't deserve Sev, or Pearla, or the sweet babe she carried. He deserved to be alone and miserable, as he feared she was, in the end.

The old house came into view. The sun was high, and sweat trickled down his temples, running down his neck and gathering at his collar. It reminded him of the hours he and his mother had spent in the fields after his father left, trying to milk sustenance out of the dry earth.

The faded blue shudders hung chipped and off their hinge, waggling in the breeze. The windows were all broken, probably having fallen victim to the games of children. Phoenix had thrown a few rocks into abandoned houses in his day, and he didn't begrudge them.

He finally stood before his mother's home…the house where he grew up.

The grass was tall, brushing his kneecaps. Phoenix saw that the structure was barely standing, leaning sharply by degrees and held up by the whims of the wind. The fields they had toiled in lay fallow; probably had done so for years.

He closed his eyes, sending a prayer to Drek that his mother hadn't starved in those days before her death. That Orin had stepped up to help where he had failed.

The spade fell from his hands, and Phoenix covered his face. The tears flowed freely; something in his chest untethered.

If he closed his eyes, he could see his mother on the porch, wiping her hands on her apron. He could see her standing in the kitchen, her dark hair gleaming before poor nutrition, sickness, and age had stolen its luster. If he concentrated hard enough, he could feel the ghost of her touch, a hand on his shoulder. She had always hated to see him cry.

"I'm sorry, Mama," he stammered. Phoenix did not have a grave to visit. This was the only memorial he had. "I should've never left. I should've never done the things I did."

He sniffed, his lips trembling. "I should've been the son you deserved."

Phoenix stood there beneath the blistering sun. He heard the screech of a bird, and a gentle wind blew across the plain. It ruffled the hair at his neck, dried the tears on his cheek.

To Phoenix, it seemed like his mother was comforting him one last time.

He stayed there until he felt better, until the tears had stopped, and he no longer felt hollowed out. He picked up the spade and made his way back down the road, leaving the past where it belonged.

Phoenix had not traveled far when he came across a wagon. The horses that were normally hitched to it were grazing in the field, enjoying their freedom. There was an old man working on the frame. Something had come loose, and the wagon had broken in half.

He walked up to them slowly, giving them plenty of time to clock his approach. "Can I be of help?" he asked them, and the old man gave him a hesitant nod.

"That's Orin's nephew," the old woman in the wagon told the man in a hushed voice. "The one who came home."

The old man waved her off. Help was help, Phoenix figured. It was getting dark, and he should see after Pearla soon. But he wasn't going to leave these two stranded on the road.

The old man had some tools in the back of the old wagon. Phoenix settled in and got to work, eager to get them on the road and get home.

◆ ◆ ◆

When the farmhouse came into view, it was already dark. Lights were on in the bedroom he shared with Pearla. Sev's light was out…she and Soren were probably already asleep.

He nearly skipped up the steps, eager to see Pearla and prepare her something to eat if she wanted.

She was in the room across from theirs.

"Hi hon," she said, her voice soft. "I thought this might be a suitable room for the baby. I've been tidying up."

Pearla took one look at his tear-streaked face, his weary appearance, and her face fell. "Are you alright?"

Phoenix offered her a reassuring smile. "I am now," he said. "Things were uh…challenging in the commons today."

She frowned and made her way to him. "I see," she said. She brushed a piece of hair behind his ear. It had gotten long. "They don't know you like I do," she said. "They don't know what a good man you are."

He kissed her cheek, lingering there. "I'll make a crib for the baby," he told her. "The most beautiful crib ever in the wide world."

She laughed. "Start tomorrow," she said. "Come to bed."

He sighed. There was still a lot on his mind. He could use a distraction. "I'll cut the boards at least, and then I'll be up."

He walked into the shed and gathered his materials. He'd lit a lantern, and the mellow glow cast a soft ambience where he worked.

It didn't matter what they thought of him, he thought with grim determination. He sawed with purpose, back and forth across the wood. His baby would have a place here, out from under the shadow of his past. He'd make sure of it.

The lantern flickered in the breeze. Tomorrow would bring more work, more planting. But the Dobani row was already in the ground. It was a start. A promise.

CHAPTER 26

Pearla was meeting Sev on her lunch break. She was in the village doing some shopping for the baby's room…new curtains, paint to touch up the trim. Pearla had an armload of packages when Sev met her at the canteen.

She took the packages from her, and they sat down to lunch. The people in the village were nicer today…friendly, even. Pearla welcomed the change, though she didn't question it.

She sipped her tea. Renna brought their lunch, setting down their plates and winking at Pearla. "I gave you a bigger portion," she whispered. "For the baby."

Sev laughed, and Pearla rubbed her growing belly. She hadn't thought it possible, but she had gotten even bigger in the last few weeks.

"The last thing I need is more food," Pearla exclaimed, and Renna smiled. "Nonsense," she said. "You're all baby. And that baby has to eat."

Pearla blushed, but took a bite of her food. She and Sev ate in companionable silence.

Sev reached for her hand and covered it with her own. "I have a surprise," she said. "I'm walking you home. Soren said I could have the rest of the day off."

Pearla grinned. "Maybe you could help me hang these curtains, then. Phoenix doesn't want me climbing."

Sev nodded, withdrawing her hand. "Don't you worry, Pearla. I'm at your disposal for the rest of the afternoon. Painting, dusting, curtain hanging. Whatever you need, I'm here."

Pearla inclined her head, warmth blooming in her chest. "I am so thankful for you, Sev. You're going to be the best big sister Lorien could ever ask for."

Sev said nothing, but Pearla could tell by the warmth in her cheek that it pleased her.

The walk home was quiet, almost pleasant, despite her aching feet. She missed transports; maybe they'd get a wagon soon.

Sev was talking to her, but she was distracted. She heard a cry, and she stopped in her tracks.

On the side of the road where they walked, tucked in a dip between two hills, was an old well.

Pearla listened for a moment, then heard it again. A plaintive cry. It sounded like an animal.

"Do you hear that?" Pearla asked Sev, and Sev stopped and listened. After a few moments, she inclined her head. "I think it's coming from the well," she said.

They put their packages on the side of the road and walked a few feet to the mouth of the well. The sounds became louder, and Pearla realized, with a chill of fear, that she had been wrong.

This was no animal. It was a low, mournful whimper.

Pearla peered over the edge of the well, down into the inky black depths. "Hello?"

There was a wail then, and a splashing sound. "Please help me!" came the small voice. It sounded like a child, cold and exhausted.

Fear gripped Pearla. She looked at Sev, where she stood in obvious shock.

"I'll go get Dad," she said, and Pearla nodded numbly. They were too far out of the village to turn back; the farmhouse was closer.

Pearla looked back into the well. It seemed to go on forever, bottomless and foreboding. "Are you hurt?" she asked.

The child sniffled. "I hurt my leg when I fell. And I'm cold. I want my mommy."

Pearla's eyes filled with tears. What if this was Lorien? She would be out of her mind with worry.

"We're getting help, love," she told the child. Pearla reached for the bucket and lowered it as far as it would go. "Can you reach this?"

There were more splashes and a few grunts of exertion. The child sniffed. "It's too high up," they said.

She swallowed, fighting helplessness. *Keep them talking,* something inside her urged. She gripped the stone edge of the well and peered down into the depths.

"Can you see me, sweetie?"

The little boy whined. "A little. But you're far away. I can't see your face."

Pearla bit her lip. "My name is Pearla," she told them. "What's your name, honey?"

The boy began crying, and Pearla listened, helpless to do anything but look down into the dark. She shushed them, and they finally stopped.

"My name is Jori," he whispered, the sound carrying up to the surface. "Can I go home now?"

Her brow furrowed. "Just as soon as we get you out, dear. Just as soon as that."

The little boy grew quiet. Pearla wrung her hands, feeling powerless there at the mouth of the well, while that poor child floundered in the dark. She closed her eyes, willing them strength.

By now, a crowd had gathered. People took turns shouting down the well, talking to Jori. The little boy was growing tired, Pearla knew. She could hear it in his faded voice, how long it took him to respond.

She heard a shout, and down the road, Sev and Phoenix were running full speed toward the well. Phoenix was carrying a long length of rope and a headlamp. He had a stricken expression on his face.

They shared a brief embrace, and she put her hand over his racing heart. "I think the entire village is here," she told him. "They all want to help. The little boy's name is Jori."

◆ ◆ ◆

It was too close to "Lori" for him not to think of his brother…his little brother he had lost to the water so many years ago. He swallowed, composing himself.

"Get me down there as quick as you can," he instructed the men. Pearla's eyes widened, and she grabbed his shoulders.

"No! Let someone else go." She gazed up at him with tearful eyes. "I can't risk losing you."

He gazed at her tenderly, then caressed her face with his hand. "What if that were our baby down there?" he asked her. "What would you say, then?"

She shook her head, knowing there was no talking him out of it. He kissed her cheek, steadying her, then turned to address the crowd. A frantic woman ran up to him, tears streaming down her face.

"That's my Jori," she said, nearly screaming. "That's my baby down there. Please."

A group of men came up to Phoenix as he was wrapping the rope around his waist. "We'll do whatever we can to help," one said.

Phoenix surveyed the crowd. His uncle was there, and many of the elders. He couldn't worry about that now.

His eyes fell on Sev and Pearla. They were holding hands, worry etched on their faces.

He finished cinching the rope around his waist and tested its strength. It was a good rope, he thought. It would hold as long as they did.

The men who volunteered grabbed the end of the rope and leaned back, anchoring it firmly. Phoenix nodded, his eyes wide. Sev handed him the headlamp, giving him a quick hug before releasing him. Phoenix swung his legs over the side of the well and walked down the first few feet.

The little boy was crying again; Phoenix could hear his muffled whimpers reverberate off the walls of the old well.

Inside, the darkness swallowed everything. The only light was the light from the headlamp, a little circle in the dark. Within its beam, he could see moss and lichen growing on the slick walls of the well. The dank smell of stagnant water rose to meet him, stinging his nose.

"Jori? My name is Phoenix. I'm gonna get you home to your mom, ok?"

Jori sniffled. There was a faint splash as he moved in the water, and Phoenix wondered briefly if the boy could touch the bottom, or if he was struggling to stay afloat.

"Ok," he whimpered. Phoenix lowered himself a few more feet, the soles of his shoes slipping on the damp stone walls. Another step, and he lost his footing, dropping too far, too fast. The men on the surface held true to his rope, but he still gasped, dislodging some dirt and rocks from the side that no doubt rained down on the little boy below.

"Sorry, buddy," he said, his voice terse. Phoenix knew he had to put the boy at ease, but that wasn't easy with as much work as it was to lower himself down in the well. "What's the first thing you'll do when you get out of here, huh? Gonna have some supper?"

The little boy hummed. "I'm hungry. And cold, too."

Phoenix frowned. The well was frigid; he could feel its icy breath permeating his clothes. He exhaled, his chest growing tight. "We'll get you a blanket just as soon as you're out of here, son. I can promise you that."

The tension on the rope creaked, and Phoenix sent a silent prayer to Drek that it held true. He was straining the limits of it with just his weight, let alone that combined with Jori's.

Finally, Phoenix felt his foot hit the water, and the little boy clamored up his leg. Relief washed over him in a breathtaking wave, causing his hands to tremble.

He huffed in relief and let the boy climb into his arms. He was soaking wet, but it was too dark to see about further injuries.

The boy coughed. "My leg hurts," he said, burying his face into Phoenix's collar.

Phoenix took a moment to comfort him before starting the precarious climb.

"Got him!" Phoenix yelled up to the surface, and he could hear the crowd cheer. The elation of reaching the boy made his head swim. It brought him back to another time, another body of water, when he had reached for his brother and had been too late.

The men called down to him. "We'll start drawing you up," one of them said, and Phoenix tugged the rope in reply.

The climb was brutal. Thank Drek for his mechanical arm, he thought…it never got tired, never trembled from over exertion. But his legs and left arm were jelly, and he was only halfway.

Mercifully, the boy did not squirm, did not move a muscle on the way up. He clung to him, frozen in fear. Above them, the light got larger, until they were close enough to pull all the way up and out.

The crowd was deafening. Soren and Sev were there with a stretcher for Jori, and they laid him down on it as soon as his mother took him from Phoenix's arms. She protested, but Soren assured her he had to be checked out first, that he had to examine his injured leg. The wagon rolled off, Jori's mother close behind, and he watched them go with a relief in his heart he had not believed possible.

Pearla's hug nearly knocked him over. She kissed him then, and he pulled away quickly. Her face was devoid of color, but the relief there was palpable.

"I'm filthy," he murmured against her skin, and she laughed.

"I don't care."

He took the rope off, and the men who helped pull him up were all looking at him with admiration in their eyes.

"You saved that boy's life," he heard a gruff voice say. He looked up, and it was his Uncle Orin.

The man had his hand out. Phoenix hesitated only a moment before taking it. Orin gave it a hearty shake.

He said nothing more. Orin gave him a brief nod and followed the dissipating crowd back into the village.

The men and women remaining stood looking at Phoenix, their expressions unreadable. A few of the younger ones clapped him on the back, smiling. The crowd parted, and Phoenix and Pearla made their way home in the dying embers of the day.

CHAPTER 27

The crops were growing. Lush seedlings were a little taller than his ankles, tender and green. It did Phoenix good to tend them while the dew was still shining on the leaves. Made his ribs spread in a satisfied sort of warmth.

He heard the clopping of horse hooves, the sounds of chattering down the road. He straightened, looking down the road, and a wagon was cresting the hill, followed by several people walking behind. They were leading two horses, beautiful chestnut steeds with long flowing manes.

The driver lifted a hand in greeting. "Hello, Phoenix!"

He returned the wave, shy and unsure; he was unaccustomed to such open friendliness from the people of Venya. Phoenix put away his spade and met them as they came into the yard, keeping to the edge of his field. Behind them, Phoenix saw some women with large baskets of goods approaching the house.

The man who'd waved to him shook his hand. "Name's Joff," he told him. He handed him a new toolbox, and the others leading the horses walked closer.

"Thought you could use some new tools, being as how you're out here on your own. And the village came together and got you these." He handed Phoenix the reins, and the horse closest to him neighed.

Phoenix rubbed the horse's nose in awe. "These are for us?"

The man quirked his mouth. "We'll help you build a barn, Phoenix." He slapped the side of the horse affectionately. "Give these two a roof."

Phoenix felt the tears on his cheeks before he realized he was crying. He never dreamed of having horses again. He hadn't ridden since he was a boy.

One villager took the reins and tied the horses to the porch in the shade. Phoenix stared, stunned. He'd need saddles. Maybe they could get a wagon, so Pearla and Sev wouldn't have to walk to the village.

Shaking off the daze, he remembered his manners. "Come inside, out of the sun," he offered, and the villagers followed him. Phoenix still felt shaken by the unexpected visit.

Pearla was already in the thick of entertaining. She had a tray of stim brew and tea, and women sat around her in the living room, talking and laughing.

She looked up as Phoenix entered. "These ladies brought me a bread starter," she said, beaming. "Herbs and spices from their gardens." Pearla withdrew something from the basket; it was a knitted cap with floppy little ears sewn on. "And the baby's first bonnet," she said with a smile.

He raked a hand through his hair, his hand trembling slightly. "Thank you," he said. "This…this means more than I can say."

Joff clapped him on the shoulder. "Thank you for what you did," he said, his eyes glittering with tears. "That boy would've died had it not been for you. We don't forget what's done for our own." He gave his shoulder a meaningful squeeze, leveling his eyes at him. "We don't let our own go lacking, either."

Phoenix swallowed and gave him a watery smile. Pearla's eyes met his, full of quiet emotion. "The girls want to give us a party for the baby," she said. "Can you believe it, Phoenix? A celebration just for Lorien."

He considered, looking around the room. The faces there were kind and warm, all trained on Pearla. And suddenly, he *could* imagine it.

Pearla smiled wistfully. "We didn't get to celebrate before…before we had to leave," she said. Phoenix watched as she blinked the memories away. It was still painful, he knew. She gave them a wistful smile. "But that's all over now."

◆ ◆ ◆

The clinic hummed with activity. Sev hurried to keep up; Soren moved with practiced ease, examining and diagnosing patients, and then sending them to her for care. Greta flitted from table to table, handing out lollipops and bottles of medicine, bandaging knees. No emergencies, just general maladies and preventative care. It was the kind of busy that felt good—productive and purposeful.

The sun streamed in through the windows. The waiting room was full. Mothers held restless children in laps, others soothed sick babies, rocking them gently. Old and young alike comprised the new clientele, and Sev couldn't be happier.

Soren caught her eye and gave her a gentle smile. He was listening to the chest of one of his older patients, a woman who'd had a persistent cough for some time.

He ran the scanner over her and read the results. Soren would use the information, plus his own exam and observations, to come to a diagnosis. It never failed to amaze her how in his element he was. She never stopped being proud of him.

"What are you thinking?" he said as the old woman made her way to her. His gaze warmed her as it always did, and she slipped her hand into his. "That this is nice," she said. "That's all."

His eyes were warm. Another patient was waiting, and the old woman needed her medicine, so he turned away.

They worked side by side for a few hours more, straight through lunch. The patients dwindled, and the waiting room finally cleared. The bell above the door rang, and a child with a cast on his leg came in carrying a large basket of fruit.

It was Jori, the little boy Phoenix had saved from the well.

"Hey," he said, evasive and shy.

Soren met him at the door. "What's all this?"

Jori grinned, some of his teeth missing. "It's a present," he said. He snatched the piece of paper off the top of the basket and handed it to him. "For you."

Soren examined it. Sev could hear him sniff, could hear his small huff of a laugh.

She walked over and examined the card. Two stick figures stood side by side. One was taller than the other, with a swath of black hair and a crooked smile. The little boy pointed to the drawing. "That's you Dr. Soren. And that's Miss Sev."

She chuckled. On the drawing, Jori had rendered her hair in yellow crayon, had given her a bright red smile. She reached down and hugged the boy. "It's perfect," she told him. "We'll hang it in a place of honor."

Soren patted Jori on the back. "You're a brave boy, Jori. Thank you for the gift."

Jori nodded, then slipped back out into the village commons. Sev took the card and tacked it on the board by the door. It looked good there, like that was where it was meant to be.

Soren was watching her fondly, and it made her stomach flutter. It wasn't unpleasant. Soren made her feel…different. She wondered, just for a moment, how she made him feel.

He held out his hand. "Ready to go?"

She grabbed the basket in one hand and gave him her other. "Let's go," she said.

◆ ◆ ◆

Pearla and Phoenix were cleaning up after their guests. Pearla had put the starter in the kitchen, somewhere warm where it would grow. She'd carefully stocked the spice rack with their spices and herbs.

Phoenix handed her a cup of stim brew and kissed her cheek, his lips lingering. "It's a beautiful evening, love. Let's go out and sit on the porch."

They settled in the rocking chairs there. Phoenix retrieved a blanket from the back of the couch and spread it over Pearla's legs. She had propped her feet up on the balustrade.

The sun was setting. The first peppering of stars was dotting the sky, day fading into night. Phoenix had set the horses out to pasture, and they grazed peacefully in the fading light. Tomorrow, Joff and the others promised to help him raise a barn.

Down the road, Phoenix spied the familiar silhouettes of Sev and Soren. His mouth quirked when he realized they were holding hands.

They stepped up onto the porch and set down the basket of fruit. Soren eyed the horses and jerked his thumb toward the pasture, his eyebrows up in question. "Yours, Phoenix?"

Phoenix's mouth quirked into a half-smile. "Ours," he said. "A token of appreciation from the villagers. Very generous."

Soren nodded. He and Sev settled in the chairs on the other side of Phoenix, and Sev copied Pearla by propping up her feet. She sighed.

"We are blessed, Daddy," Sev said, her voice tinged with something quiet, something reflective. Phoenix reached for her hand, giving it a little squeeze.

"I'm a charmed man, to be sure, to have such a family."

"And friends," Pearla added.

Phoenix could scarcely believe it. "And friends, too."

CHAPTER 28

The days passed in a blur of warmth and quiet satisfaction. Each morning, Phoenix checked the crops, marveling at how well they responded to the Venyan sun—tall, strong, already budding. He heard from the villagers how well Soren and Sev were doing at the clinic; they seemed to fit right in. The village trusted them, and it showed.

Pearla seemed more radiant by the day. Phoenix noticed the way she cradled her growing belly with both hands now, her movements slower, more deliberate. She went to the clinic often, under Soren's insistence. Soren swore he'd keep a watchful eye on both her and Lorien, and so far, he'd kept his promise.

Venya had been kind of late. There was no telling how long their luck would hold, though, so Phoenix clung to these moments.

The barn stood half-finished—just beams and walls for now—but Sev had already decided that was where the celebration would be. He'd found her just this morning draping garlands over the frame, balancing on a stool and humming to herself as if the party had already begun.

Villagers arrived with baskets filled with flowers, cider, sausages strung like garlands, and rounds of cheese. Joff barked orders from a hay bale and handed Phoenix a roll of bunting, pointing him toward the rafters like he was commanding a building crew.

Soren brought out a rocking chair from the porch and positioned it inside the barn. He added a bale of hay for Pearla to prop her feet on and stepped back, arms crossed, studying the setup with the same focus he gave the rest of his patients.

Later, Phoenix climbed down from the ladder and spotted Pearla deep in conversation with Renna near the refreshment table. She wore one of the new frocks the village women had sewn for her—colorful, flowing—the fabric stretched lovingly over her belly. A flower sat tucked behind her ear.

Children darted between the adults, shouting and laughing, weaving beneath bunting and half-hung banners in a frenzied game of tag. Phoenix leaned against the ladder and took it all in, letting the moment settle deep in his chest.

◆ ◆ ◆

Pearla watched Renna leave, looking around the barn for Phoenix. She brightened when she saw him, and he opened his arms to her. He pressed a kiss to her cheek, lips hovering over her ear.

"You're more beautiful today than the first day I saw you," he whispered, and her cheeks flushed with color. She pulled away from him, stars in her eyes.

"I don't feel that way," she said, eyes roving over his face.

He gave her sides a gentle squeeze. "Well, you should. It's true. Motherhood suits you."

She narrowed her eyes. "Don't get any funny ideas, Phoenix. Sev is the only sibling Lorien is ever going to have."

He chuckled, caressing her face fondly. "I better get back to work. Joff is a merciless taskmaster."

It made her laugh as only Phoenix could. She sat back down in the rocker. Soren caught her eyes from where he was helping wrangle the children, and he motioned for her to put her feet up. She sighed; indeed, they were swollen and sore.

Guess it's a blessing to have a doctor in the family, she thought, as much as he pestered her.

Sev flitted between the refreshment table and Soren's games with the children. Pearla watched her play with them, and it warmed her heart. She was going to be such a good big sister.

A string quartet was setting up in the corner. Pearla recognized the leader from the village, and he gave her a kind smile. Music soon drifted through the barn, clear and bright.

Soren grabbed Sev's arm, giving her a spin. Pearla watched them for a moment. Sev had her head thrown back, and she was laughing. Soren watched her with unmistakable warmth. It touched something deep within Pearla to see them both so happy…two children, really. They'd both been through so much.

Greta clapped her hands. She was standing in the middle of the barn a few feet from where Pearla sat. The music faded as heads swiveled toward her.

"It's time, everyone. Pearla is going to open her presents now. And then you're free to dance and eat and just enjoy yourself."

Sev and the children brought her package after package until they piled on either side of her.

She looked around, at a loss for words. She'd come here as a refugee, a stranger from a ruined land. And these people embraced her and her family. She was so unspeakably grateful.

Sev saw her struggling and brought her a tissue. "One at a time, dear Pearla," she whispered. She kissed her cheek and handed her the first package, giving her a bright smile.

Pearla blew out a breath. People were sitting in chairs watching her. Some were standing by the refreshment table. In the corner, Pearla saw Phoenix's Uncle Orin holding a plate of food.

She carefully peeled back the paper and untied the string.

Phoenix chuckled from across the barn. "We'll be here all day if you're that mindful, dear heart." He was standing with the other men, a cup of cider in his hand. "Rip it open!"

Everyone laughed. She opened the next gift with more enthusiasm now, and she couldn't deny that it felt good.

The paper fell away in a flurry of wrapping, and she opened the box. A handsewn stuffed rabbit lay within. It was patchwork, made up of different colored squares.

"Oh, my goodness," Pearla cooed. She held it up, and a collective sigh spread throughout the barn.

Renna beamed. "That one is from me," she said shyly. "I finished it just yesterday."

Before she could linger, Sev handed her another. She peeled away the wrapping, revealing a beautifully carved rattle.

Pearla gasped. The whittling was intricate, from a skilled hand. She gave it a little shake, listening to the sound. "Who gave me this? It's so beautiful."

No one answered right away. Phoenix caught her eye, holding up his glass of cider. "That one's from Uncle Orin," he said, a fond smile on his face. "Made it himself."

She searched the crowd for him, but he was nowhere to be seen. He must've left early.

Pearla clutched it to her chest. Of all the villagers who had come around to them, Uncle Orin's acceptance meant the most. Perhaps because it meant so much to Phoenix.

After a few more presents, Soren stepped forward. He had a wrapped box in his hands, and he handed it to her.

"This is from me and Sev," he said, and she hurried to open it. She popped open the lid, and Soren spoke again.

"It's not sentimental," he began bashfully, "but it's things every first-time parent needs."

She withdrew the first aid kit carefully. There was a thermometer, a scanner, nail clippers, and an array of tonics for sick babies. Lotions and powders. Ointments. Her chest tightened with emotion. Soren was looking after Lorien even now.

Phoenix gave him a nod from where he stood. "That was thoughtful, Soren. And I know we'll put it to good use."

Pearla agreed. "Thank you," she told him, then looked at Sev. "Both of you."

The party wore on. After Pearla opened all the presents, Joff presented Phoenix with a gift of his own…a tiny farming set, complete with rake and spade, but toddler sized. "You gotta train 'em up early," Joff told him jovially, and it coaxed a chuckle out of Phoenix.

After everyone had eaten and had dispersed to various corners of the barn holding their own discussions, Phoenix approached Pearla, his hand outstretched. "I don't suppose I could trouble you for a dance," he asked, suddenly shy.

She blushed but held out her hand for him to help her up. The quartet was still playing, and music floated soft and melodiously through the barn. He led her to a space cleared for dancing and pulled her close.

Pearla laid her head on his chest as much as she could with the baby between them. With their height difference, it fit right under his chin, and she felt safe—tucked in. Phoenix held her hand in one of his, and the other wrapped around her lower back.

"This was so nice," Pearla murmured. She was tired from the day's activities, but it felt earned rather than draining.

Phoenix hummed. "Perfect," he whispered, though she wondered if he was talking about just the party. "You haven't asked what I got you yet."

She laughed. "You've already given me so much, Phoenix. I don't expect a present."

He dropped a kiss on the top of her head, swaying gently to the music. "It's in the shed," he said simply.

They danced until the sun set and all the guests had gone home. Sev and Soren had moved the baby's presents into the house and returned the rocking chair to the porch. The women had put away the food, packing up the leftovers and storing them in the kitchen.

Phoenix led her by the hand to the shed, then moved behind her. He covered her eyes with his hands.

"No peekin'," he cautioned her, and she laughed.

He made her count backwards from three. When she got to one, he leaned in close. "You ready?"

She gave a soft nod, her hands covering his where they blocked her vision. He removed them, and the last of the evening light poured in.

Phoenix had completed the crib. It stood under the shed, varnished in a natural finish. The ends were etched with delicate flowers and twining vines. He'd carved the word "Lorien" in careful script.

Her throat tightened. Phoenix could always find beauty in the simplest of places. It's one thing she loved about him, and it was clear in the beauty he'd pulled out of the wood, his careful carving.

He'd also built shelves, a changing table, all in that natural finish, all etched with flowers. In the middle sat a gliding rocker, complete with cushion and footrest.

"Oh, Phoenix," she gasped. "It's all so perfect." She held his hand, the pressure of his palm against hers a reassuring presence. "When did you have time to do all this?"

He shrugged. "I did it for you, my love. And for Baby Lori."

He wrapped his arms around her; they no longer met over her belly, but he didn't seem to mind. One by one, the stars came out, and the deepening blue sky faded into black. They walked back toward the farmhouse, holding hands.

CHAPTER 29

The morning was golden. Phoenix couldn't remember a more beautiful day—a perfect day. Today, more than any other, he wanted everything to be just right.

He'd been up before the sun, brushing the horses until their coats gleamed.

Sev walked out onto the porch with her stim brew, her hair pulled back in a messy ponytail. She still wore her pajamas.

"What are you doing up so early, Daddy? I just weeded the garden yesterday."

He gave her a fond smile, putting away the brush. He patted the horse on the flank and walked up to the porch to sit with Sev. She'd taken a seat in the rocker there.

"And I thank you kindly, little mouse." Nervously, he looked down at his hands. "I wanted to talk to you about something."

She took a sip of stim and locked eyes with him. "Of course, Daddy. You can tell me anything."

He breathed in, gathering his courage. "You know…that I love Pearla, right?"

Sev gave him a soft nod but said nothing.

"And I love you. So much, Sev. And of course, I respect your feelings."

She reached over and laid her hand atop his. "What's this about, Daddy?"

"I wanna ask Pearla to marry me," he blurted out. "But I wanted to ask you first. If that would be ok with you."

He looked at her hopefully, his heart in his throat. Then he saw her eyes light.

"That's the best thing I've heard in a long time," she said, and he felt the anxiety in his chest release by degrees. "And I know just the place."

◆ ◆ ◆

Pearla woke up to Sev serving her breakfast in bed. She'd prepared eggs and warm toast, porridge and ham. Off to the side sat a small dish of sliced fresh fruit.

Pearla blinked awake, roused more by the delicious aroma than the sun sifting through the curtains. She struggled to sit up, and Sev put a pillow behind her back.

"What's all this, hon? And where's your father?"

Sev waved her hand. "He's doing chores. He's taking you on a picnic today, Pearla. Have a little breakfast, and then I'm going to do your hair."

Pearla rubbed the sleep from her eyes. "A picnic? Where?"

Sev unfolded her napkin and placed it delicately over her baby bump. "It's a surprise. Now eat up. I'm going to get things ready. You are royalty today," she said with a wink.

Pearla frowned. She didn't know what was up with Sev, but if she knew her, she wasn't likely to figure it out anytime soon.

◆ ◆ ◆

After breakfast, Sev sat Pearla down in front of the mirror. She had an array of products, a curling rod, and makeup in front of her. The sun shone through the gossamer curtains of Pearla and Phoenix's bedroom. Her belly comfortably full from breakfast, Pearla relaxed into the moment.

Sev brushed Pearla's azure hair straight, then wrapped a portion around her curling rod. When she released it, it sprang into a delicate curl.

"Do all women in your family have such colorful hair? I never thought to ask."

The mention of her family stung a little. She had not heard from them since Dobani fell, something that was never far from her mind.

Pearla covered Sev's hand where it rested on her shoulder. "Blue is the predominant color, but there are others. And usually our eyes match."

Sev ran her fingers through the silky strands. "It's beautiful. You know, Daddy was taken with you all those years ago, when you came to help us clean up after the storm. He kept talking about how nice that 'blue-haired woman' was."

Pearla giggled. "I'm glad I could make an impression," she said lightly.

Sev leaned in close. "Oh, you did, sweet Pearla. I'm so happy you're a part of our family."

Pearla rubbed her hand over her stomach. "Our growing family," she reminded her.

Sev just hummed.

◆ ◆ ◆

Phoenix dressed well, like he was going into the village. He didn't want to propose in farmer's coveralls. He swept his hair back, taming the cowlick now more grey than white. Some days, he couldn't believe he was going to be a father again.

And now a groom. He knew they were doing things a little backwards. He should've asked her ages ago. Phoenix only hoped Pearla could forgive him for waiting so long.

Pearla came out onto the porch wearing a new spring dress, her hair coiled in an intricate style. Sev had applied her makeup, though it only augmented her natural beauty.

Phoenix held out his hand, a little awed by her. "Let me help you into the wagon, my dear," he told her. She gave him a radiant smile, and his stomach flipped.

He was so nervous already. Phoenix wondered how he'd find the courage to ask her.

He got her settled in the wagon. Sev brought out the picnic basket, tucking it in the back. He waved to her, and she gave him a little wink.

Pearla frowned. "What was all that about?" she asked him.

Phoenix shrugged, keeping it casual. "Oh, you know Sev."

Pearla seemed satisfied by that. He held the horse's reins, and she covered his hand with hers.

"Thank you for this," she murmured, and his heart clenched.

"I haven't done anything yet," he said, and she gave him a soft smile. She laid her head against his shoulder, and they rode the rest of the way in quiet companionship.

◆ ◆ ◆

Around lunchtime, they arrived at the glen. Green grass and wildflowers stretched along the banks of a sparkling stream. In the middle of the water, there was a little island with a single tree. Flowers dotted the grass.

Pearla stared, awestruck. Even Phoenix had to pause at the sight. He made a mental note to thank Sev and her excellent planning. This was the perfect spot.

Phoenix helped her down off the wagon and looped the basket over his arm. In one smooth motion, he picked her up in his arms and waded into the shallow part of the stream.

Pearla squealed. "Put me down this instant!" she half-laughed. "I'm too heavy—you'll throw your back out."

He hefted her easily and walked the few feet to the island. He gently set her on her feet. She was still smiling; the sun was filtering through the dappled leaves of the single tree and painting her face in strokes of light.

Phoenix unpacked the basket and withdrew a blanket. He spread it under the tree and patted the space beside him.

He helped Pearla sit down, as nothing was easy as pregnant as she was, and he leaned back on his elbows. Only the stream, the wind, and nearby birdsong broke the stillness.

"Hungry, my love? I have snacks. And cider."

He poured them both a glass, holding his up. "A toast," he announced.

She watched him, her eyes as blue as the sky. "What's the occasion?"

He clinked his glass with hers. "Us," he said. "Isn't that enough?"

♦ ♦ ♦

After a while, she ended up with her head in his lap, and he silked his fingers through her hair.

"I hate to mess up Sev's careful work," he said fondly, "but I can't help myself. You are a precious pearl, indeed."

She closed her eyes. Phoenix swallowed hard. It would be so easy to lose heart here at the penultimate moment. To spend a few more hours languishing on this idyllic island and go back to the farmhouse, nothing changed. It would be so simple.

He frowned. It would be a copout, and she deserved better.

He continued stroking her hair, her eyes still closed. She appeared to be asleep, but he knew she wasn't. Phoenix dug into his pocket, closing his fist around what he found there. He pulled his hand out, keeping it beside him.

"Pearl," he whispered, and she opened her eyes. "Can you, uh, can you listen to me for a minute?"

She smiled, warm and curious. "I always listen to you, Phoenix." Then she narrowed her eyes, appearing concerned. "What is it?"

"I want to ask you something," he said quickly before cowardice took over. "Something important."

Her mouth twitched into a frown. She was thoroughly concerned now; he could tell. "Ok. Phoenix, you're scaring me."

His eyes watered, and he blinked away the unexpected emotion. He thought briefly of his mother, of what she would think of him now. Of what she would say.

"Pearla, my dear. Mother of my child, love of my life. Will you be my wife?"

She gasped, her hand going up to cover her mouth where she still lay in his lap. He offered her his hand, and he helped her sit up. She gazed at him with wet eyes, and he withdrew what he'd been concealing.

He opened his fist, and inside there was a ring. It was a carved wooden ring, polished to a shine. Leaves and branches twined around it, intricate and decorative.

She held her hand out, and he looked at her expectantly.

"So…is that a yes?" he asked, his voice a little watery.

Pearla laughed, a breathy thing. "Yes, you wonderful, silly man. A million times, yes."

She wrapped her arms around him, kissing him. Phoenix's chest swelled with warmth, and he felt lighter, freer than he had ever felt. He was getting married. He was going to be a father.

Phoenix withdrew and slipped the ring on her finger. It was a perfect fit.

She held up her hand, admiring it. "It was my mother's," Phoenix said. "Uncle Orin gave it to me."

He watched her study it, watched the color bloom in her cheeks. "It's beautiful," she told him. "It's perfect."

Phoenix wrapped his arms around her. They sat under the tree for what seemed like ages until the birds stopped singing and a cool wind blew over the water.

He rubbed her arms. "Let's get you home before you catch a chill," he told her.

Once again, Phoenix carried her through the shallow stream. It was ankle-deep, at most, and was frigid where it had trickled down from the hills.

Phoenix helped her onto the wagon and covered her legs with the blanket. The horses were restless, so Phoenix shook the reins, and the wagon lurched forward, rolling along the rural road toward the farmhouse.

CHAPTER 30

Sev stood by the window, watching the rain hammer the glass. She'd heard that this kind of weather wasn't unusual for the season, but the sheer force and relentlessness of it felt excessive.

Greta scurried around the clinic, mopping up leaks. She'd placed buckets and bedpans under the largest ones. A persistent drip flowed steadily in the corner; the pail catching the rainwater was nearly overflowing.

When she wasn't keeping things dry, Greta was helping wrangle patients. Children sat bundled in layers, coughing and shivering. Elders filled the waiting room, the rainy weather tendering their joints. It was a busy day at the clinic, but not unexpected.

Greta walked the next patient back to the exam room, leading the little girl by the hand. Her mother trailed behind, nervous and fussing over the child.

Soren sat her down on the exam table. Sev was close by.

"If it keeps raining like this, I'm closing up early," Soren said offhandedly. He was systematically checking the girl's ears and throat. She was a good patient, calm and pliable.

Sev chuckled. "Good. If we miss dinner again, Daddy's going to ban us from the clinic."

He looked over and gave her a gentle smile, his eyes warm. Sev knew Soren had attached himself to this place and the people here. There was no extricating him now.

Thunder rolled in the distance. The world outside was as grey as Kedros, and the mere association gave her a shiver.

Suddenly, Greta came rushing in, a holopad in her hands. There was a haunted look on her face. She laid it down on the exam table beside them without preamble and pressed the button.

Soren straightened, lowering his instruments. Sev walked up beside him as the holopad winked to life. A villager they knew stood in the rain, soaked to the bone and holding his hat on his head against the wind.

"Pearla's having pains, and the bridge is out! She and Phoenix are trapped at the farmhouse!"

Sev nearly dropped the scanner she was holding. She looked at Soren, and his skin went pale as moonlight. He turned to her, his eyes fierce with purpose.

"Sev, get the bag. Check that it's stocked—double check. Greta, take over seeing patients and close early. Then go home and get some rest," he said, a hand on her arm.

Sev checked and re-checked Soren's black bag. She'd packed a scanner, clamps and scissors, and other supplies that might be useful. And there was a scalpel, in case it came to that.

They had prepared for this. Pearla's time was near, she knew. But it couldn't have happened on a worse day.

Soren grabbed her by the arm, and they plunged into the rain. The downpour soaked them immediately, chilling her and causing her to shudder. Sev sent a silent prayer up to Drek for Pearla to hold on, for little Lorien and for her father, who must be out of his mind with worry.

They made their way out of the village. It was dark and getting darker, with the sky crowded with storm clouds.

Up ahead, Sev saw the remains of the bridge jutting from the bank, and beyond that, a rushing river. Her stomach dropped. A crossing here meant being swept away, lost in the flood. Pearla might die. Lorien too.

Soren seemed to read her mind. He held her wrist, tugging her gently. "Miller's farm," he nearly yelled against the torrent. "The crossing there is narrow. Maybe the water's not so high."

She licked her lips, considering. It was their only option, really. It would take more time, but that was unavoidable now. She set her mouth and followed Soren off down the bank.

The crossing wasn't too far across, but the water was higher than normal from the swollen river. They stood looking out over the water. Sev's eyes were wide and a little fearful.

She turned to Soren. His face was resolute, and as usual, he exuded quiet calm. Sev envied that about him. She felt like panicking, but she knew that wouldn't solve anything.

He grabbed her hand. "Don't let go, Sev. Whatever you do. We can't get separated." He searched her eyes for understanding; the chill had drained what little color remained from his face until his skin was pearlescent, like the face of a moon. She squeezed his hand in answer.

Carefully, he led them out into the river.

The current pushed against her, almost knocking her off her feet. Each step was a battle, struggling against the current as Soren pulled her along. *For Pearla*, she kept thinking. It helped keep her focused.

They were halfway across. The water was waist-high and getting deeper, and she struggled to keep her footing. They were both hypothermic, she knew. They needed to warm up, but that wasn't happening until they got to the farmhouse.

Soren never let go of her hand. When they finally scrambled up the muddy bank, Sev took a moment to catch her breath. She was shaky with adrenaline and trembling with cold. She lifted her head, and Soren was staring at her.

He placed a hand on her shoulder, applying gentle pressure there. "We must go, Sev. We have to hurry."

She followed him down the road. It was not long until the farmhouse, but it had been at least an hour since they'd received the call. Pearla might've had the baby by now. Or, she thought darkly, she might be in real trouble.

After a while, the farmhouse came into view. All the windows stood dark. Sev realized with dread that they must've lost power.

Soren bounded up the steps, and together they burst through the front door. It was dark inside, but warm. Dry. That, at least, was a comfort.

"Pearla? Dad?" Sev called up the stairs. She half-expected to hear a baby's cry, but she didn't. Only a moment later, she heard her father's voice.

"Up here, Sev!"

Soren looked at her, his face tense with intent. "Get some fresh towels and meet me in their bedroom," he said. "Go, Sev."

She hurried to gather the items, the bag still looped over her arm. She rushed upstairs and walked through the open door of their bedroom.

Her father had lit candles and oil lamps, and they glowed all around them, providing soft light. Pearla lay propped up on the bed, her face flushed and drenched in sweat. Tendrils of hair stuck to her ruddy cheeks, and her brow was tight with pain. Phoenix sat beside her, his hand in hers. His eyes appeared haunted and betrayed a fear she was not used to seeing there.

Soren had already shifted gears. His wet hair dripped in his face, but his hands were steady. He looked up at Pearla and gave her a little smile. "Time to push, Pearla. Take a deep breath, and then push on the exhale, ok?"

Pearla gave him a jerky nod. Phoenix appeared stricken as he looked on. Sev handed him a cold cloth, and he mopped her brow, trying to make her more comfortable.

Pearla pushed, grunting loudly, her eyes shut tight.

Phoenix tutted. "You're doing so well, my love. You're so strong."

Soren agreed. "That was good, Pearla. Just a minute, and we push again, ok? Just a few more. You're doing fine. More than."

Pearla deflated after pushing, exhausted from her labor. Sev's chest clenched to see her so distressed. Phoenix rubbed her shoulders and down her sweat-soaked arms. They were trembling.

"Get the women," Pearla murmured weakly. "Renna promised to help."

Soren patted her gently. "It's too late for that, Pearla. You're too far along, and the bridge is out. It's just us now."

Pearla frowned. Sev watched as a new determination settled on her face. At Soren's word, she prepared to push again.

Sev crossed to the other side of the bed and gripped her free hand, trying to imbue her with strength.

Pearla pushed. Pain carved deep lines into her face. The thunder rumbled outside, and lightning split the sky. A sudden, sharp cry broke through the storm, and Soren brought baby Lorien to his chest.

Sev gasped. She grabbed a clean towel, and Soren laid the baby in her arms.

Lorien was beautiful—pink and wriggly and loud. The baby had a swath of dark hair. Sev swaddled Lorien tightly and handed the bundle to Pearla.

"Oh, sweetheart, oh my goodness," Pearla cooed, cradling it close. The baby settled, finally comfortable in its mother's arms.

Phoenix wept, overcome.

Soren smiled at him, his eyes shining. "It's a girl, Phoenix. You have another daughter."

He had a hand to his head, and he stared at Lorien with unbridled affection and more than a little shock. The baby had her eyes closed, her little pink hand close to her face.

"Let me see her," he murmured gently. "Let me see my little girl."

Pearla handed the bundle to Phoenix, and he brought her in close. Sev watched with tears in her eyes as her father met his newest daughter.

"Hello little one," Phoenix whispered. "Look at you, how beautiful you are. How perfect, hmm?" He swayed gently, and the baby made little mewling sounds, her dark eyes focused on her father's face.

Soren was cleaning his hands. He had some color back in his face, and his eyes glittered with tears. "You were wonderful, Pearla," he said to her. "But you need rest now. Let us help."

She lay back on the pillow, her eyes still on Lorien where Phoenix held her, a soft smile on her face. She nodded and closed her eyes.

The storm had passed. Evening sunlight broke through the clouds, pooling in the puddles outside.

CHAPTER 31

The early morning sun warmed the farmhouse. With the windows open, the curtains billowed softly in the cool wind left from last week's rain. Pearla slept, having fed Lorien off and on through the night. Phoenix held his daughter in his arms, walking her through the house, his steps light.

He took the bottle he'd warmed on the stove and brought Lorien to the nursery. He sat down in the glider rocker he'd crafted, the sun through the windows dusting everything in a golden aura.

Lorien grunted and gave a single cry before Phoenix could get the bottle to her mouth. She sucked hungrily, and it made Phoenix smile. His girl had a healthy appetite.

He ran a fingertip along her cheek, marveling at her soft skin. Lorien reached for it, clutching it in her tiny hand.

"Eat up, little one," he told her gently. "Later, after your bath, we'll walk in the garden. I can show you the crops, the rest of the farm." He caressed her dark head with his hand, easily cupping her entire head. "I can't wait to show you the world, Lorien."

She blinked up at him with large, glassy eyes, almost like she was listening. She seemed unusually alert, though Phoenix knew little about such things. He remembered his brother Lorien being fussy, how his mother jostled him at night just to get him to sleep. So far, his girl had an agreeable temperament, and he was immeasurably grateful.

Lorien drained the glass bottle, and he set it aside. Phoenix put her on his shoulder, just as Soren had shown him, and patted her back. The resulting little burp felt earned.

He put her in her crib long enough to prepare a basin of warm water. From there, he gave her a gentle wash, soft bubbles floating on the surface of the bath, then dried her off with a fluffy towel. Lorien fussed, angry at being taken from her bed, and let out a sharp wail. Her face was red, her little button nose scrunched. Phoenix found it all very endearing.

After her bath, Phoenix dressed his daughter in a soft new tunic, marveling at the size of it. It was so much fun seeing the clothes they'd received at the party finally worn by his doll-sized daughter. Phoenix enjoyed dressing up Lorien almost as much as Pearla did.

When she was clean and dressed, Phoenix swaddled her tightly and sat back down in the rocker. Lorien was sleepy; her little eyes blinked slowly, and her mouth opened in a slight yawn. Soren had told him that babies slept a lot. Phoenix gave her his finger to clutch, and she readily took it. He hummed the only lullaby he knew, a song he'd sung for Sev long ago. She'd always found it soothing.

"There you go, darling girl. Time for a nap now," he whispered.

Phoenix closed his eyes. He'd been up most of the night checking on her. He drifted off too, holding Lorien close to his chest.

◆ ◆ ◆

Pearla found them sometime later, both asleep in the rocking chair. She smiled, warmth blooming in her chest. She stood over them, careful not to wake Phoenix. His head lolled against his shoulder. The little streak of white in his hair had fallen over his forehead.

She gently took her daughter in her arms. Phoenix had dressed her; she was wearing a new tunic and little knitted socks. He'd swaddled her in the blanket she had made.

Pearla laid Lorien in the crib, soothing her when she fussed at being disturbed. She bent to kiss her on the head. On her way out of the room, she bent and kissed Phoenix on the forehead, too.

Sometime later, Pearla was in the kitchen preparing breakfast, and he came up behind her, pressing his lips to her cheek. "You should be resting."

Pearla laughed. "Nonsense. I feel fine. Soren said it's good for me to be up and moving." She covered his hand with hers. "Something tells me your new daughter doesn't abide either of us being too lazy."

He gave her a reassuring smile. "Not lazy, my love. But rest while you can." He set the table, humming softly. "I fixed Lorien more bottles. They're in the fridge for her feedings. And I did a wash."

Pearla turned off the burner and moved the pot of porridge to the table. "You did all of that while I was asleep? Hon, maybe you should go lie down, now. You should rest too."

He chuckled. "I just woke up. Besides, I want to spend time with you while it's just us. While our little one is sleeping."

She blushed and settled at the table across from him. Phoenix reached across the tabletop and threaded his fingers through hers. They ate in companionable silence, both listening, half focused on the soft sounds beyond the door.

◆ ◆ ◆

After breakfast, Pearla and Phoenix prepared to go into the village commons. Some diligent villagers had repaired the bridge, opening the way for traffic. Soren wanted Pearla to come into the clinic for a thorough check-up, and Sev had agreed to come in and stay with Lorien.

Sev had never been alone with a baby.

It wasn't that she was afraid; Sev felt secure in her ability to care for Lorien and keep her from harm. The trepidation came from the memories stirred just by being around her.

When she was very young, Sev had begged Del for a sister.

It was irrational, she knew, the whims of a small child. Del grew impatient, ordering her to stop. But her heart yearned for a playmate all the same.

It would've been unfair to the child for Del to bring another innocent into their dangerous nomadic lifestyle. Sev knew that now. But it didn't stop her from grieving the fact that she spent her childhood mostly alone.

Later there'd been her books and writing. Her music. But no playmates. No siblings.

Sev knew she was a little old to miss something she had never had, but that didn't stop her from feeling whole when she looked at Lorien. Looking at her felt like closing a circuit—like something long-missing had finally clicked into place. She finally had a little sister. There were two of them now.

Sev saw her father and Pearla off in the wagon, promising to look after Lorien with the utmost care. She could feel the worry exuding from them, the separation anxiety. She shook her head in amusement, wandering toward the nursery to check on her ward.

Lorien was lying in her crib, hands flailing gently, watching the wooden mobile that hung there. She cooed when she saw Sev, her dark eyes brightening.

Sev picked her up, swaddle and all. "Hey there, Sissy," she whispered. She jostled her gently, creating a slight rocking motion. "I sure do love you, little girl." Her eyes prickled with tears, and she blinked them away. "I used to go to bed at night with a prayer for you on my lips."

She smiled wistfully, and the baby gazed up at her. Lorien gave her a toothless grin, and Sev touched her chin with the tip of her finger.

Sev walked her into the living room and settled with her on the couch. Her father had dressed her in a soft little tunic with socks. Phoenix loved dressing up his girl.

Lorien looked up at her with dark eyes. Sev couldn't decide who she resembled most—she had her father's hair, minus the white patch, but Pearla's coloring. Soren had told her that babies' eyes were always blue at first, and then they changed. Sev lowered her head and kissed Lorien's forehead. She inhaled deeply, breathing in that fresh baby smell. She wondered if Lorien's eyes would turn brown, like Phoenix's.

It didn't bother her that they weren't blood related.

She shared no blood with Phoenix, either—she'd learned long ago that family was more than that. Family was who stayed when you were sick. Who celebrated with you. Who sometimes cried with you. Family was who made you feel like you belonged.

Lorien was just as much her sister as Phoenix was her father, and she loved her just as fiercely.

After a while, the baby began to fuss and wiggle, so Sev took her upstairs to the changing table. She laid her gently atop it and stared in mild trepidation at the various implements: the cloth diapers, the pins, the powders. For a second, she considered calling Soren to talk her through it, but she resisted. She'd flown to Terra Firma and back. She'd space-walked with no backup. Surely, she could handle this.

And she did. Lorien, to her credit, was as cooperative as a baby could be.

After the change, Sev carried her back to the living room and cradled her on the couch. The room grew warmer with the sun through the windows, and Sev dozed in and out to the sound of Lorien's soft breathing—until the distant rattle of wagon wheels signaled that her family had returned.

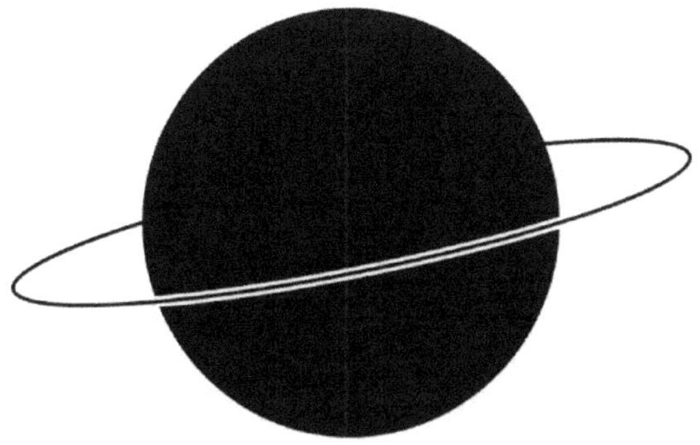

CHAPTER 32

Languid days and nights stretched into weeks. Crops in the field were heavy with a summer harvest, vegetables hanging on their stalks ripe for the plucking. The rain had cleared and had not returned, save for the brief evening shower.

The harvest would have to wait. Today, the village was celebrating. It was the wedding day.

In the barn, villagers strung tiny fairy lights and white bunting. They'd brought in tables and chairs, and the ladies had pressed cloth over the smooth surfaces there, adorning them with centerpieces of candles and bundles of dried flowers.

Sev stood behind Pearla, brushing her hair. Sev wore a long, flowing gown with little flowers embroidered on the hem. Her hair was partially up, accentuating her face.

Renna fussed with Pearla's dress. It was pale blue with embroidered sleeves. Little colored flowers dotted the neckline, drawing the eye up. The waist was tapered and fitted; Sev didn't know how Renna and the other girls had gotten the dress done to Pearla's usual measurements while she was still pregnant, but the dress fit her perfectly. Pearla was beaming.

"Are you excited?" Sev asked her, pulling the comb through her wavy hair.

Pearla made a face. "I'm nervous. But yes, excited too."

Nearby, Lorien cooed, and Sev laughed. Sev had dressed her in a little white tunic with soft leather shoes. Lorien kicked and played in her bassinet, her hand going up to stretch in the sunbeam coming through the window. She fisted the air as if she could grab it.

Sev kissed Pearla's cheek. "Don't be nervous, Pearla. Everyone will be there for you. Supporting you. And you look absolutely radiant."

Renna agreed. "This dress, the way it matches your hair and your eyes. It's perfection." Renna squealed. "Oh, I just love weddings!"

Sev watched the woman leave in a rush, amused. Pearla looked up at Sev, a wry grin on her face. "I think she's more excited than I am."

Sev laughed, as did Pearla. It broke the tension, and Sev gave her shoulder a little reassuring squeeze. Pearla sighed, covering Sev's hand with hers. "Thank you," she breathed, "for everything."

◆ ◆ ◆

Soren waited outside the bathroom, pacing in the same beam of light from the window that he'd traversed for the last few minutes. He checked his chrono, then nervously raked a hand through his hair.

"You ok in there, Phoenix?" he called at the door. "It's been a minute. You don't want to leave Pearla waiting."

Finally, the door opened. Phoenix had water dripping from his face and down the front of his new tunic. The collar sat askew, and his hair was in disarray.

"Did you dunk your head in there?" Soren asked him, half joking.

Phoenix gave him a tight shrug. "I may have splashed my face a little," he said abashedly. Soren frowned. Phoenix was pale, and his hand trembled.

"Come here," Soren told him, and Phoenix walked over to him. Soren blotted his tunic with a towel, then gave it to him to dry his face. "How do you feel?"

Phoenix frowned. "Sick," he admitted. "Even my nerves have nerves. How am I going to get through this?"

Soren sighed. "You love Pearla, right?"

Phoenix brightened. "More than anything. And I want this," he assured him. "It's not that I don't."

Soren narrowed his eyes. "What is it, then?"

Phoenix looked down. "I'm not sure. I think it's the ceremony…the big deal everyone's making. If it was just us, I'd be fine."

Soren reached out and straightened his collar. He grabbed a flower and pinned it to his tunic, right above his heart. He pressed his hand there, letting it linger. "You're going to be fine, Phoenix. More than. Once you see Pearla, all those nerves will disappear."

Phoenix took a breath, smoothing the front of his tunic with his artificial hand. "I guess we'll see," he said with a little laugh.

◆ ◆ ◆

Sev was in the kitchen, helping with the food. There were trays and bowls of fragrant dishes, rows of sweet cakes and various desserts. She snuck a bit of fruit from one tray and popped it into her mouth, trying not to look like she was starving.

"I won't tell if you won't," she heard a playful voice say. She pivoted toward the voice, and it was Soren. He was looking at her, one hand in the pocket of his slacks. Soren had dressed to stand with Phoenix; he looked sharp in his suit.

He walked toward her, a soft smile on his face. "You look beautiful, by the way. You may outshine the bride."

A furious blush stained her cheeks, and she couldn't stop the smile at his words. "Thanks," she said, trying to sound casual. "You look good too. I mean nice. You look nice."

She swallowed, wondering why she sounded so ridiculous. Not knowing what else to do, she offered Soren a piece of fruit. He politely declined.

"How is Pearla?"

Sev gave him a gentle smile. "She's nervous, honestly, but excited. And Phoenix?"

Soren laughed. "He's an absolute mess. He dunked his head in the sink."

182

Sev giggled. "You're lying."

Soren held up his hand in a solemn pledge. "Hand to my heart, that's exactly what happened."

"Before or after he got dressed?"

Soren smirked. "After. Wet the entire front of his tunic."

Sev huffed. "Poor Daddy." Then she giggled again.

She looked up, and Soren was staring at her. "What is it?" she asked him.

He shook his head. "Nothing. I mean. I love it when you laugh. That's all." He looked embarrassed, and she almost regretted asking him.

Her mouth quirked up. "What's gotten into you?"

Soren shrugged. "Must be the wedding," he said cryptically.

Renna stuck her head into the kitchen, her eyes wide. "You two ready to move these dishes to the barn? It's almost show time!"

Sev gave him a shy smile, and they seemed to snap out of it. "Of course, Renna." She looked at Soren, and he was already moving to help. "We'll get these where they need to be. Is Pearla ready?"

Renna hummed. "Ready or not. The sage will be here soon. Joff's been seating everyone." She clapped excitedly. "We're about to have a wed-ding," she said, all sing-song.

She walked away, and she and Soren shared an amused smile.

The village sage stood under the old willow tree. Soren was a serene presence by Phoenix, his hands folded in front of him. The villagers sat in white chairs; they'd all dressed in their best and looked at him expectantly.

He'd calmed down considerably since his last breakdown. But that was only a few minutes ago.

The quartet started, and soft music floated over the arbor. A gentle wind blew over the crowd, carrying with it the sweet smell of summer. Sev stepped out onto the porch and walked down the steps there, and his stomach dropped out.

His oldest daughter was so beautiful. She had a flower crown in her hair and carried Lorien in her arms. As she got closer, he realized his youngest had on a tiny flower crown too, nestled in her dark hair. She was looking up at Sev, content to be held. Sev was smiling at him; she looked so proud.

Tears stung his eyes, and he pinched the bridge of his nose. Phoenix watched Soren as he looked at Sev, unabashed fondness on his face. It settled his nerves, knowing his Sev was cared for so.

The music swelled, and everyone stood. Pearla floated out into the yard, her pale blue dress catching the sun, her hair flowing behind. She wore a flower crown too, and she held a bouquet of fresh flowers.

The tears came freely now; she was the most beautiful thing he'd ever seen.

Pearla was smiling as she joined him in front of the sage. She handed off her bouquet to Renna and reached for Phoenix's hand.

And just like that, all his nerves dissipated. He took his first full, deep breath of the day and locked eyes with the mother of his child.

The sage addressed them, and then the crowd. Lorien fussed, and Sev lovingly shooshed her, bouncing her against her shoulder. His daughter gave a shrill shriek, and some villagers laughed.

"Are you prepared to exchange vows?" the village sage asked them.

Phoenix nodded, then remembered he was supposed to speak. "We are," he belatedly said, and Pearla offered him an encouraging smile.

He lowered his head, looking at their joined hands, and swallowed his nerves.

"Pearla," he began, his voice watery, "You came into my life offering help, all those years ago. Something so simple as cleaning up after a storm. But you helped me in more ways than that. You gave me my daughter back. Pearla, you've given me years of love and companionship. You accepted Sev as your own. And now, you've given me yet another reason to love you…sweet little Lorien. Our shared jewel."

His voice wavered, and he looked into her eyes, seeking the strength there. "I want to be worthy of your love, my Pearl. Every day I want to earn your devotion."

Soren handed him the simple gold band, and he took it in a shaky hand. "Take this ring as a symbol of my vow to be the husband you deserve."

He slipped the dainty band on her finger. She was crying, delicate tears streaming down her face. He admired the way the ring looked alongside her engagement ring. The metal and wood together exemplified Pearla perfectly…her softness and strength.

Pearla took a breath, gathering herself. "You're a wonderful man, Phoenix. Kind. Strong. So giving. You gave me the family I never knew I wanted." She glanced over at Sev and Lorien, a gentle smile on her face. "I vow to be the wife you deserve and will work every day to be worthy of your love."

She sniffed, and Sev handed her Phoenix's ring. It was wider than hers, with intricate etchings and an inscription within. "Take this ring as a symbol of my vow."

She slipped it onto his finger, and Phoenix huffed a laugh. They were both crying now. Lorien cooed, kicking her feet, and Sev kissed her head.

The sage recited a Venyan blessing, and the audience recited it back. She smiled at Phoenix. "Phoenix, you may kiss your bride."

Phoenix wasted no time. He leaned forward, cupping his new wife's face, and kissed her reverently.

The villagers whooped. Soren clapped Phoenix on the back, congratulating him. Pearla reached for Lorien and took her from Sev. The little girl squealed at being back in her mother's arms, and Phoenix laughed.

Joff stood in front of the assembly, his arms spread wide. "There's food and music in the barn," he announced. "Everyone, please stay, eat, and enjoy. We've much to celebrate."

Phoenix and Pearla followed everyone to the barn. He couldn't stop smiling, and he brought his hand up periodically to stare at the gold band on his left hand. Pearla shoulder-checked him playfully. "Guess you're stuck with me now," she said with a wry grin.

He met her eyes, a soft smile on his face. "Happily," he said. "I'm happily stuck."

They entered the barn, and it was glowing with fairy lights. White silk bunting hung from the rafters, and green plants with long vines twined along the walls. The barn glowed with soft light; pleasing music floated throughout, and the succulent aroma of food dwindled in the air. Pearla handed Lorien to

Renna, who promptly fussed over the child, drawing a crowd of several other villagers. Phoenix grabbed Pearla's hand and led her to the dance floor.

◆ ◆ ◆

Soren watched Phoenix and Pearla with a gentle smile on his face. It was such a genuine moment, and he couldn't have been happier for them.

He sat at the table, a plate of food in front of him. He wasn't that hungry. From across the room, he watched Sev talking and laughing with a villager.

She was so beautiful. He had told her as much before, in the kitchen, but he had downplayed it to not make her feel uncomfortable. She caught his gaze, and she gave him a shy smile.

How one little gesture like that could feed his soul, she would never know.

Soren picked at his food, trying to stimulate his appetite. He felt someone sit down beside him, and he turned his head. Of course, it was Sev.

She studied him, her seafoam eyes questioning. "Not hungry?"

He swallowed. "I guess not," he said nervously. Part of her hair had fallen out from around her flower crown, and his hand itched to push it back behind her ear. He flattened his hand on the table, squelching the desire.

"Do you want to dance?" he blurted out, and her mouth fell open only slightly. Her eyes softened then, and she gave him an affirming smile.

"Sure," she finally said, and he thanked whatever deity was looking out for him for the lifeline they'd thrown him.

He gathered her hand gently in his and led her to the dance floor. The quartet struck up a soft, melodious tune, and he gently wrapped his arm around her, pulling her close.

She watched his face, eyes searching, and he smiled. "You're not bad," he murmured, and she laughed.

"Gee, thanks for the ringing endorsement," she said playfully, and he shook his head.

"No, I meant that you're a good dancer," he amended.

It made her lips quirk. "You are too. You dance much back on Ocarro?"

He averted his eyes. Ocarro seemed like a lifetime ago. "No, nothing like that. Spent most of my time in school. Long hours studying."

She let herself imagine Soren when he was her age. "No girlfriends? No dances?"

He blushed and shook his head. "No, Sev. I was too busy trying to become a doctor for anything like that."

She tightened her arms around his neck as they danced. "Look at you now, though. Guess it all paid off."

He said nothing. She laid her head on his chest, and he closed his eyes. When he opened them, Phoenix and Pearla were right beside them, regarding them fondly.

"Mind if I cut in?" Phoenix asked him.

He smiled and released Sev to her father. Soren then asked Pearla to dance, and she accepted with a wink.

♦ ♦ ♦

Phoenix took his daughter in his arms, spinning her gently. She laughed, looking up at him like she had when she was just a young thing.

"You know how much that boy cares for you, right?"

Sev flushed. "Daddy—"

"Uh uh. None of that. Just as long as you know."

Sev said nothing, and he pressed on. "You know how much I love you, Sev. Whoever wins your hand will have to love you just as much, if that's even possible."

She gave him a soft smile and lowered her eyes. Phoenix pulled her in close, gently swaying them to the music.

"Is he good to you?"

She met his eyes, nodding once.

Phoenix smiled. "Ok then. That's all I needed to hear."

He dipped her, and she squealed with laughter. "What do you think of your old man being married, hmm?"

Sev grinned. "I think it's long overdue." They said nothing for a while. "I'm proud of you, Daddy."

He kissed her on the forehead. "Thank you, little mouse. I'm proud of you, too."

◆ ◆ ◆

The dance continued for a few songs, then both couples departed to their respective tables to wait on the cake.

They celebrated into the night. Lorien got passed around like a little doll until finally she grew fussy, and Renna took her inside for a bottle and a nap.

Sev and Soren escaped from the barn to take a walk under the starry sky. He led them down the road a bit, past the ripened fields and the little stream that ran parallel to the farmhouse.

"I'm so happy for them," he said. To him, it sounded like a confession. Sev said nothing, and he took her by the hand. "I'll never stop being thankful for your family taking me in, Sev. For welcoming me as one of them."

She gave him a soft smile, the moonlight catching her flaxen hair and casting a glow across her serene face. "Of course you're one of us," she said. "And we always look out for our own."

He squeezed her hand, his thumb grazing over her knuckles. "We better get back before they send a search party," he quipped.

Sev threaded her fingers through his. "A little longer won't hurt," she said shyly, and they walked on toward the stream.

◆ ◆ ◆

It grew late. The barn emptied, and the villagers put away all the leftovers. They promised to come back tomorrow and remove the tables and chairs, the bunting and lights. Phoenix sat on the porch with his new wife. Lorien slept just inside, nestled in her bassinet, close enough that they could hear her if she cried. He watched down the road where Sev and Soren had disappeared a while ago.

Pearla grabbed his artificial hand, giving it a squeeze. "Want me to go find them?"

He lifted her hand to his mouth and pressed a kiss atop it. "No dearest. They're fine."

As if he'd summoned them, he heard laughter coming up the road. Sev was holding her shoes in her hand, bare feet padding on the hard-packed ground. She and Soren were holding hands.

They walked up on the porch, all smiles. Sev bent to kiss her father on the cheek, then Pearla. "I'm going upstairs to get a shower," she told them. "Today was a wonderful day."

Pearla caught Phoenix's eye, giving him a glowing smile. "Indeed, it was," she said. "We've much to celebrate."

Soren clapped Phoenix on the shoulder. "Congrats again." He regarded him, his face suddenly serious. "It was an honor to stand with you today."

Phoenix grabbed his arm, clasping it. "The honor was all mine," he said fondly.

He watched them walk back into the house. Behind them, Lorien fussed. He took his feet down where he had propped them on the balustrade, and he and Pearla walked into the farmhouse together.

CHAPTER 33

The sun was warm on their backs as they bent in the fields. It was not yet midday, and the soil was still tacky with overnight dew. Birds called to each other, flying overhead. Sev was not sure how her father had kept the crows off the harvest, but the vegetables were whole and unfettered. She had a basket of them already, and she wasn't halfway down the row.

"We've a bountiful crop, little mouse," Phoenix said to her. He was working on another row, but farther down than Sev. "Drek has blessed us with food enough for sharin'."

Sev hummed her assent. She was sweaty and tired, but it was the nice sort of exhaustion that came from a job well done. She'd been digging purple tubers…seeds her father had brought from Dobani. He'd surprised her with them only a few weeks ago.

"We'll have to invite the village. They can help with the harvest if it becomes too much."

Up ahead, Phoenix looked back at her, a wry grin on his face. "Tired of farming already, little mouse?"

She laughed. "Tired, but not fed up." She gave him a gentle smile. "I'm happy, Daddy."

And indeed, she was. She felt more settled than she had in a long time. They'd carved out a place for themselves here. It felt right.

Prescott agreed. "I'm releasing her at noon," he said matter-of-factly. "She's not sick, not going to be sick. And you're right, Pearla. Her place is here."

♦ ♦ ♦

Pearla was folding the last load of laundry, the house sun-warmed and cozy. Lorien lay in her crib wearing a summer jumper, kicking and cooing. Pearla hummed as she worked and intermittently stole brief glances at her daughter where she played. Lorien was listening with large eyes, ever attentive.

Her holopad pinged, and she furrowed her brow. Pearla crossed to activate it and waited for the grainy image to materialize.

She held her breath. The face was hazy, then more concrete. It was one she feared she would never see again, and the relief nearly stole her breath. The woman's blue hair blended with the hologram's usual pall, appearing white. Pearla's eyes filled with tears.

"Mom? Is that you?"

The woman's face split into a smile. "Darling Pearla! I feared I would never see you again."

Pearla was openly crying now; she ached to wrap her arms around her mother, now that she knew she was alive. "Mother, how—"

"Dobani is liberated, Pearla. You, Phoenix, and Sev can come home again."

Pearla swallowed. The news was so unbelievable to her…that they could return home. That they could live on Dobani and be happy once again.

The transmission flickered. "The generator is running out. There's no power. Most of the infrastructure is down. But they are rebuilding. We are rebuilding."

Pearla thought of Lorien. Her mother had never seen her. "Please, don't go yet, Mom. There's someone I want you to meet."

She stood and gathered Lorien in her arms. The little girl squealed, giving her a gummy smile. She played with her mother's hair, content to tug it gently as Pearla carried her over to the holopad.

She settled in front of it. "This is your granddaughter, Lorien," Pearla told her with tears in her eyes. "Lorien, say hi to Grandma."

Lorien flailed her arms and kicked her feet, enamored by the holopad image. On screen, Pearla's mother was crying.

"Oh Pearla, I can't wait to hold her in my arms. My heart is full."

Pearla held her daughter close. Sitting there, presenting her to her mom, felt like closure. It felt like healing.

"When can—return?" her mother asked, the audio becoming distorted. The image wavered once more, then it winked out.

Pearla sat back on the couch with Lorien in her arms. Her little girl's coos and babbles were the only thing keeping her grounded in the moment. The news had overwhelmed her, but so had seeing her mother for the first time in many months.

When she'd gathered herself, she stood and walked out onto the porch. She saw Sev in the field, but not Phoenix.

"Sev!" she called to her, and the girl looked up from her task. "Get your father and come inside. You both need a break."

She could see Sev straighten and stretch her back. She called to her father, and they dropped their tools and walked back to the house together.

Phoenix came in first, skin dewy with sweat and hands dirty. He leaned in for a kiss, and Pearla wrinkled her nose. "Go shower, and I'll fix lunch. There's been news from Dobani."

He stopped in his tracks, his eyes wide. "What news?"

She hurried him out. "Go, both of you. Wash quickly and I'll tell you."

Truth be told, she didn't know how.

She'd believed her mother dead…had grieved for her even. And Dobani, she understood, was lost. How could this be that they were getting a second chance to go home? By the time Phoenix and Sev met her in the kitchen, she was still unsure what to say.

"Dobani is emancipated," she said, the words coming out in a rush. She grabbed Phoenix's arms. "We can go home again."

Phoenix searched her face, then finally gave her a big smile. "Lorien can learn to walk on Dobani soil," he exclaimed. He reached over and put a hand on Sev's shoulder. "Little mouse, did you hear that? Dobani is free."

Sev gave him a prim smile but said nothing. Pearla noticed she was unusually quiet but thought nothing of it. Perhaps she was tired from the field or overwhelmed, just as she had been.

Pearla turned to her, tears in her eyes. "Isn't it wonderful, Sev?"

Sev hugged her then, resting her head on her shoulder. "It is, Pearla."

♦ ♦ ♦

After lunch, Phoenix went to the village commons to use the information kiosk there. He had to find out for himself the news of Dobani, of its liberation.

What he found quickened his heart.

Dobani had pulled together and pushed out the invading forces. They'd liberated their people on Kedros and other camps and brought them back home. Dobani was free. Dobani had been victorious.

It filled him with pride and hope both. He couldn't wait to get there. He could scarcely wait to see their home, to settle Lorien into the little nursery he'd built. To give her the toys he'd bought her that still sat in the closet.

When he got home, he called everyone together. Soren was home from the clinic, and he came out of the kitchen, wiping his hands on a dish towel. He'd helped Pearla prepare dinner, but it was still in the oven. Phoenix sat with Lorien in his lap and Pearla beside him. Sev and Soren settled on the other side of the low table there.

"We'll need to leave after the harvest. We can split the bounty with the villagers since we won't need to winter here. Pack the necessities, but pack light. We can get what we need when we get home."

Sev looked down at her hands. Soren was similarly quiet.

"The horses can go back to Joff…Drek knows he's been good to us. And Venya has been good to us. But home is home."

He cooed at little Lorien, waggling his fingers, and she laughed. Pearla sat beside him, a hopeful smile on her face.

Sev frowned.

"I can sell off the wagon," Phoenix continued, "and Renna can have her property back. It will be like—"

"I want to stay."

Phoenix stopped talking and looked up at Sev. Soren was watching her in profile, but her eyes were fixed on Phoenix. "I want to stay here, Daddy. I don't want to leave."

A knot formed in Phoenix's throat, and his chest felt tight. "What do you mean, sweetheart?"

Sev blinked away tears. "I mean, I think my place is here right now. At the clinic. With these people."

Phoenix looked from her to Soren. He could scarcely believe what he was hearing. He swallowed, and his voice sounded thin when he finally spoke. "And you?"

Soren reached for Sev's hand. "I'll be wherever she is," he said, resolved.

Pearla had covered her mouth with her hand, and she looked over at Phoenix. He met her eyes for a moment, reading the shock there, then handed Lorien over to her.

"Alright then," he murmured, standing as if to walk away. "I uh, I need to go get some things together." A muscle ticked in his jaw. "I'll be down a little later."

But Phoenix never came downstairs. The supper finished cooking, and they ate without him. It was a solemn affair, with Pearla trying to cajole conversation out of Sev and Soren. Sev was unnaturally quiet.

Pearla's heart twisted. She'd come to think of Sev as a daughter, too. But she understood. She really did. That didn't make it any easier.

Soren and Sev offered to do the dishes, and Pearla went to take Lorien upstairs to the nursery. Before she could leave the kitchen, Sev called her back. She approached her and wrapped her in a warm hug.

"I'm going to miss you, Pearla," Sev said softly. "Thank you for always being there for me."

Pearla blinked back tears. "I love you, dear Sev. Like you were my own."

She pulled away before Sev could reply, patting her gently on the arm and turning to go upstairs with Lorien.

Once in the nursery, she gave Lorien a bottle and tucked her in, winding up the mobile above her bed before she left.

She found Phoenix sitting on the edge of the bed, looking lost.

Pearla sat down beside him and put her arm around his waist. "We missed you at supper," she tried.

He shook his head. "I can't believe she's not going with us," he whispered. "She doesn't want to go home? I don't understand."

Pearla frowned. It had hurt Phoenix, she knew. She could feel the heartbreak, could see the conflict in his face. She placed her hand on his cheek.

"Sev is making a new home, Phoenix. And she's old enough to forge her own path. You know this."

He angled away from her, unwilling to hear it.

"She's my little girl," he said miserably.

"And she will always be." She caressed his face. "Let her fly free for now; she'll eventually return."

He hung his head, looking at his folded hands where they lay in his lap. "I hope you're right," he told her. Then he looked at her, a soft smile on his face. "I guess I know you're right."

Pearla rested her head against his shoulder. "You know how much she loves you," she said.

Phoenix hummed. "That's why this is so hard."

◆ ◆ ◆

Phoenix woke up feeling better. Pearla had talked to him long into the night, reassuring him that Sev wasn't abandoning her family…that she was just making her own decisions, and that was a sign of healthy growth and maturity. It still hurt, but he loved her. Drek, did he love her.

He walked into the kitchen for some much needed stim brew, and Soren was sitting at the table there. Sev must've still been asleep.

He gave him a smile and poured his own steaming cup. He walked over to the table but did not sit down.

"Let's take a walk, Soren," Phoenix said.

He led him down the drive toward the field, stim brew in hand. Halfway there, he stopped, sunlight just beginning to streak the horizon.

"I'm going to say some things, and I want you to just listen."

195

Soren swallowed and gave a quick nod. He had fixed his eyes on Phoenix, the dark irises gone to grey in the morning sun.

"I know you care for my daughter very much. When I leave, you'll be responsible for her well-being. Sev is a capable girl…strong beyond my comprehension…but she still needs love. She needs looking after."

Soren was listening—that much he could tell. "If you ever can't give her what she deserves…put her on a transport to Dobani." He looked at him squarely in the eye.

"Don't call. Don't write. Just send her home where I can take care of her."

He looked down, then back up at Soren. "Don't you ever, ever hurt her. Do you understand?"

Soren nodded. "Yessir," he said, a little belatedly. "Can I…can I talk now?"

Phoenix chuckled. "Yes, you can talk."

Soren cleared his throat. "You're right. I do care for Sev. Deeply, in fact. And you have my word: she will never come to harm while she's with me."

He took a deep breath. "And I want to thank you for letting me be a part of your family." He offered his hand. "You've been good to me, Phoenix, and I'll never forget it."

Phoenix shook his hand. "Ok then, son. You take care of my little girl."

Soren gave him a smile. "You have my word."

◆ ◆ ◆

With Sev and Soren staying behind, there was far less to do. Phoenix and Pearla packed; they would leave the horses and wagon and let Sev decide how to divide the crops with the villagers. Her father was folding the last of Lorien's clothes and pressing them into a small duffle when she caught his hand.

He met her gaze, his eyes filled with tears. "Don't know if I can leave you, sweet girl. You're one half of my heart."

She pulled him close, tears in her eyes. "I hope you understand my decision," she whispered. "I love you so much, Daddy. But I'm needed here. Soren and I are making a difference. And that's more important than what I would do on Dobani."

She pulled away, her glittering eyes catching her father's. "That's the only reason."

And she realized that was true. Here, she'd found purpose and opportunity. On Dobani, she would've returned to school, and what then? It seemed so trivial.

"Don't be a stranger," he murmured. He smiled a little sadly. "Little Lorien needs her big sister."

Sev held both his shoulders, looking at him squarely. "She'll have me," she promised. "And so will you." She averted her gaze, worrying her bottom lip with her teeth. When she looked back, there were fresh tears in her eyes. "Just give me a little time to get things settled here. Then, I'll follow you."

Phoenix gave her a gentle smile and pulled her close. After a few moments, Sev pulled away, studying her father's comforting and familiar face as if committing it to memory. She dug into her pocket and withdrew the blue calcet.

"We never needed it," she mused. "Though I don't think I could've given it up, anyway." She pressed it into his open palm. "This is Lorien's. Take it home where it belongs."

He closed his hand around the gem. Behind Sev, Pearla came in with Lorien. "Are you ready, Phoenix?"

He nodded, his eyes distant. "Yeah honey. Let's go home."

Phoenix went to where he'd loaded the wagon and slung the duffle bag he was carrying in the back. He held up his hand to his oldest daughter, and she returned the gesture. Soren walked out of the house to stand by Sev and raised his hand in farewell, too.

Phoenix said nothing else. He climbed onto the wagon and spurred the horses onward down the drive. He did not look back.

Sev stood and watched her family retreat in the dust kicked up by the wagon long after they were gone. She felt a longing in her heart, a hollowed-out space that was not there before they left.

Sev turned to Soren. She was on the verge of tears, her lips trembling slightly. She had the sudden urge to chase the wagon, to hop into the back of it, and to take Soren with her.

Soren touched her arm, reading her mind. "What do you feel in your heart, Sev? I only want you to be happy. Like I said before, I'll go wherever you go, clinic or no."

She smiled, and Soren reached up and caught one of her tears with the pad of his thumb before it could fall. Sev gave him a soft nod. "I just want to do the right thing," she finally said.

He grinned, a little lopsided. "Do we ever really know what that is?"

It made her laugh, and she immediately felt better. She tugged his arm. "Come on, let's go back inside."

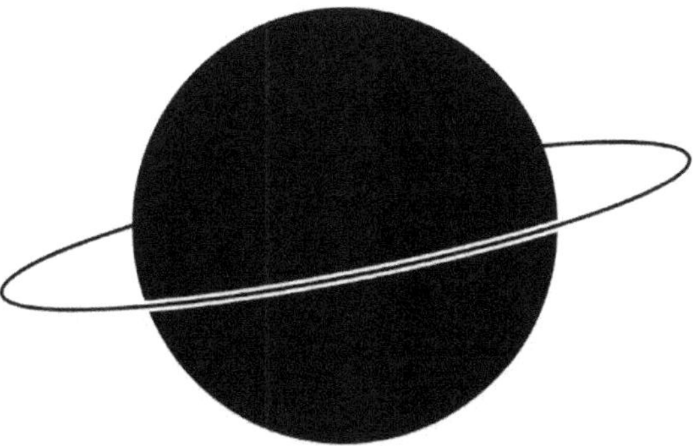

CHAPTER 34

Stars blurred outside the small oval viewpane of the transport. The overhead lights were low, creating a calm and pleasant atmosphere for space travel. For being in the Black, it was about as comfortable as you could be.

Phoenix looked over at Pearla. Lorien was asleep on her shoulder, and she was resting up against his arm. This time, they weren't stowaways. They weren't refugees. They were passengers on their way home. More than that, they were survivors.

Not for the first time, he thought of Sev—the daughter he was leaving behind. He was still torn about his decision. Should he have forced her to come with them? Or should they have stayed and left Dobani in the halls of their memories?

He leaned his head against the viewpane, feeling its grounding chill. Beside him, Pearla cradled their daughter like a blossom. He had to be sure he was doing the right thing. There was too much at stake, otherwise.

Phoenix must've drifted off, because when he woke up, the transport operator was making an announcement. Landing was imminent; passengers needed to strap in for touchdown.

Pearla was feeding Lorien, looking down on her with a gentle smile. Phoenix reached out and caressed Lorien's foot, and the baby jerked her leg, probably ticklish. Phoenix grinned. "Our girl is hungry today."

Pearla hummed. "Hungry every day. Like her daddy."

Phoenix laughed. It dissipated some of the anxiety he'd been feeling about leaving Sev, but he still wondered what awaited them planetside.

They didn't have to wait long. They docked at the Terminal on Dobani and made their first hesitant steps on familiar soil. Only it wasn't familiar at all.

Mortar holes pockmarked the Terminal. Exposed beams barely held the walls up; there were charred and scarred surfaces everywhere. Security doors opened and closed on their own.

It was eerily quiet within. Shell-shocked citizens returning home wandered aimlessly through the Terminal as if not knowing where to go next. Phoenix checked his punchcard at a kiosk and breathed a sigh of relief when his old credits were there. One less thing to worry about, he thought. He grabbed Pearla's hand and pulled them toward the exit.

They stood on the sidewalk waiting for a transport. Pearla looked around, fearful eyes wide. "This does not feel like home," she said, holding Lorien tighter in her arms.

They got the first transport available. The exterior was littered with graffiti, but the operator had cleaned the inside. He was pleasant, welcoming them back. "It's not the Dobani you remember," he said glibly. Phoenix agreed.

He and Pearla looked out of the viewpanes on their way out of town, stymied by what they saw.

The road was unrecognizable. Gutted buildings stood half-fallen, ready to topple at any moment. The hulls of transports smoked on the side of the road. They'd burned a learning center, and Phoenix briefly wondered if Sev's school had been spared.

He guessed it didn't matter now.

The only recognizable thing was the little sliver of ocean he saw in the distance. Sev's ocean, he mentally amended. He could almost see her as a child, browning in the sun, chasing crabs across the sand.

Once again, he wondered if he had done the right thing.

An hour later, they were turning into their drive. Lorien was fussy and overdue for a nap. Traveling so far with a baby had proven difficult.

Up ahead, the palms in the yard still stood proudly. It gave Phoenix a brief flash of hope that he would find that all was well.

The transport pulled up in the front yard, and Phoenix craned his neck to see.

The front door was off its hinge, swinging open in the breeze.

Pearla gasped. She must've seen what he was seeing. Both bay windows stood shattered, the glass barely in their frames. He stood on wobbly legs and unloaded the transport, leaving what little they'd brought in the yard for now.

A neighbor crossed the street and stepped across the drive, his arm outstretched.

"Good to see you back, Phoenix. Guess it'll take more than an occupation to get rid of us, eh?"

He slapped him on the back, and Phoenix managed a good-natured laugh. It was good to see that people were trying to get back to normal, at least.

They made their way inside the house. It was dark within. Pearla covered Lorien's head protectively, and Phoenix wondered briefly if she should be in there at all.

The house was a wreck. It appeared to have been used as some sort of barracks. Ration bar wrappers lay strewn throughout; empty canteens and bedrolls filled the corners. Trash and general disrespect littered his home. A half-collapsed tent slouched in the middle of the living room.

"Oh, Phoenix," Pearla said, gasping. "Where do we even start?"

Phoenix had no answer. He turned to Pearla and saw Lorien reaching for him, her fingers grasping the air. He gave her a gentle smile and took his little girl into his arms.

Down the hall, he peered through the open door of Sev's room. Her journals and books were scattered, and her bed was off its frame. It made him sad to see his daughter's belongings treated so. Anger flared within him, but he tamped it down.

Across the hall was the nursery. He braced himself and pushed inside.

It was miraculously untouched. The galaxy still shined on the ceiling, and the model of the skiff stood dusty but undisturbed on the dresser. Lorien's crib stood waiting for her, blanket and all. For the first time since their return, something felt right.

Phoenix brushed off the dust and laid her down on her bed.

He dusted his hands, looking around. It was bad, but not insurmountable. They had to start somewhere.

Phoenix wandered back out to the living room where Pearla was already working to get things in order. She turned to him, smiling.

"I heard from my mother. I told her we were back home, and that we would come to the Highlands as soon as we could. She wants to meet Lorien."

Phoenix wrapped an arm around her. "Of course she does. She's going to spoil her properly, I just know."

Pearla nestled against his chest, and Phoenix stroked her hair. "It's been a long journey," he murmured. "Why don't we do just enough to get things passable for tonight, and we'll start fresh in the morning, hmm?"

She looked up at him, a soft smile on her face. She wiped her hands on her skirt, taking a deep breath. "Sounds good."

Pearla trailed off toward the kitchen. The invaders had plundered all the cabinets, leaving the doors swinging free.

"At some point, I'll need to go into Dobani Proper. See what's left of the shop."

And suddenly, as if she just remembered. "And Emma! Oh, poor Emma. I hope wherever she is, she's ok."

Phoenix placed a hand on her arm. "I hope so too, Pearl. I'll help you with the store. Whatever needs to be done, we'll do it."

Pearla started in the kitchen. Phoenix discarded the old tent and cleaned out the corners of the living room, keeping an ear out for Lorien. When he checked on her a little later, she was asleep.

Phoenix looked down at his daughter's angelic face, relaxed and at rest. He thought of Sev, a star system away. He felt every mile.

But in his heart, he trusted her to make her own decisions. His Sev was smart and more than capable and so full of love. He knew that whatever path she chose would keep her close to her roots.

He came out of the nursery, down the short hall, and into the living room. Phoenix stood among the refuse, his hands on his hips. The nursery was intact, and the beach still glittered in the distance, but there was work to do here to make this house a home again.

CHAPTER 35

Sev opened her eyes to the soft mid-morning light streaming through the sheer curtains of her bedroom. The only sounds were birdsong and the gentle rustle of wind moving through the trees.

She lay there in bed, listening to the deafening quiet. There was no crying baby. No Pearla and Phoenix laughing at the kitchen table. The old farmhouse felt still now, like a spark smothered before it could catch.

She sat up slowly and swung her legs over the side of the bed. The floor was cool beneath her feet, the boards smooth from years of tread. She pulled on her robe and walked to the window. The sun was bright, the trees a brilliant summer green. It reminded her of Terra Firma. She thought of her time there more and more in recent days.

She gathered her robe around her and padded down the hall, eager for a cup of stim brew.

Before she went downstairs, she paused at the nursery.

The furniture was still there. The changing table, the little dresser. Her father hadn't taken it—too bulky for the transport. They'd decided at the last minute to leave the crib behind, and it now sat empty in the pale light.

Sev rocked it gently, imagining her sister curled inside.

She would miss little Lorien's first steps, she thought ruefully. Her first words. The first time she reached for her, soft eyes sparkling.

Sev sat down in the rocker, her hand still on the crib. Unbidden, tears stung her eyes. Some part of her insisted she belonged with them. That she was an integral part of the village that would raise Lorien.

Absently, she traced Lorien's name her father had carved lovingly into the wood. She thought of her sister's namesake, of her Uncle Lorien. She wished she could've known him. Sev wished he and her father could've grown up together, and that her father had not had to bear the burden of poverty alone.

She closed her eyes. *Am I failing him?* she wondered.

She stood and meandered around the room. Her fingers drifted over the dresser, smoothing her palm over the varnished top. She opened a drawer, and there, tucked in the corner, was a tiny, knitted sock. She picked it up, rolling it between her fingers, imagining the little foot it had once held. A weight settled in her hollowed-out chest. Did she remember the last time she held her?

Before she could grow maudlin, she gently set it back where she'd found it.

Her throat tightened, but no tears came. Her family was not gone; they were just somewhere else. Still a part of her life. Always would be.

She flipped off the light and closed the door softly behind her before heading downstairs.

The kitchen was quiet. Soren had already made stim, and it sat steaming in the pot on the kitchen counter. Again, it shocked her how still everything was. The kitchen, with its scarred table and aging appliances, looked like a museum diorama, frozen in time.

Sev poured herself a cup and sipped it gratefully. Through the window, she saw Soren sitting on the porch, his feet up on the balustrade. Just like her father used to do.

She pushed through the front door and joined him outside. He had a small bowl of fruit in his lap.

He looked over at her with a soft smile. "Come have breakfast with me," he said in lieu of a greeting.

But her mood was low. She grabbed a slice of melon from the bowl and bit into it, the juice bright and sweet on her tongue. She took a sip of stim and leaned against the railing, gazing out at the field where the horses grazed beyond the garden. They whinnied intermittently, swishing their tails in the morning sun.

"How long have you been up?" she asked.

"Couple of hours," he replied easily.

Sev frowned. "We're going to be late to the clinic. I bet the waiting room's full already."

Soren took another sip and offered her the bowl of fruit. "That's why they call it a waiting room, Sev," he said wryly. "They can wait a little while."

She laughed, and it felt good. She'd felt contemplative since she first woke up…her feelings jumbled and thoughts racing. There was still no word from Phoenix, and she could scarcely wait to hear from him.

As if reading her mind, Soren reached out and touched her arm lightly. "Heard from home?" he asked her, and he said it so easily it was like Dobani was his home too, despite him never having been there.

She inclined her head. "They said they would reach out once they got settled," she told him.

Soren pressed his lips into a smile. Sev knew he was trying…that he could tell she was feeling off.

"He will. You know your dad."

Sev gave a wistful smile. "Yeah," she said, warmth rising in her chest. She did know him. Better than she knew anyone, she imagined.

◆ ◆ ◆

She was right; the waiting room was packed, and the patients were restless. Sev and Soren offered hurried apologies as Greta smoothed tensions with cups of stim and distractions on the holopad.

Sev settled into the flow of work. It was comforting…familiar. Her mood lifted, and she lost herself in habitual actions.

Soren was setting a broken arm while Sev helped an older woman review her prescription. She explained the dosage instructions gently, reminding her to finish the entire bottle.

From across the room, Soren caught her eye, a soft smile playing on his face. A familiar warmth blushed her cheeks, fluttered beneath her ribs, and she managed to smile back before turning to apply the plaster cast for the next patient. They worked in tandem, wordless, slipping in and out of each other's cases like practiced dancers.

Sev realized at that moment that she and Soren were no longer outsiders. They were part of this place—integral and familiar. Not refugees. Not transient. They belonged.

It filled in a little of that hollow feeling that had been present ever since her family had left for Dobani…that sense of belonging.

The day wore on. The last folder disappeared into Greta's satchel, and Soren scrubbed his hands at the sink. Outside, stars peppered the deepening sky. Sev collected her things and waited by the door. As usual, Soren reached for her hand.

Even with the wagon, they always walked home.

Their boots trod over the path until the farmhouse came into view, warm light glowing from the windows like welcoming eyes.

Soren headed for a shower. Sev followed him upstairs, diverting toward her room and rifling through her books and papers.

She pulled out her journal. It was dusty from disuse, and she brushed off the film that had collected on the cover. Sev hugged it to her chest and went back downstairs.

She made herself a cup of tea, the sound of Soren's off-key humming drifting from the bathroom. It made her smile.

With tea in hand, she settled on the couch, folded her legs under her, and opened her journal for the first time in a long time.

Sev had gone through many journals over the years. Phoenix had bought her most. When she was younger, before she'd met Phoenix, she'd purchased notebooks from scrounged credits, or from bartering with Del. He never bought her one. He loathed her writing…found it wasteful and frivolous.

Sev opened the journal to the first page and looked at the entry there, dated almost two years prior. She shook her head. Had it really been that long? Her fingers brushed over the indentions of her writing on the soft paper, the brightly colored ink a little faded with time.

She was fifteen. It was her birthday.

Sev read the entry, choked with tears. She'd been so happy. Phoenix had given her a picnic on the beach and gifted her a telescope. The entry recounted the bright pink paper he'd wrapped it in. There had been no box, so the long cylinder betrayed the gift immediately, yet Sev never let on that she'd figured it out. She'd acted surprised when she'd peeled the paper off, revealing her heart's desire.

Pearla helped her set it up. They took it down to the beach that night and looked at the moon. Sev mapped the craters there and observed the bright, pale glow of its surface. She was just getting to know Pearla then. Her thoughts of her recorded in her journal were reserved…cautious. She had no way of knowing then that Pearla would become one of her dearest friends. Pearla became that soft female presence that Sev had always hungered for.

Sev took a sip of her tea and flipped to the last entry. She'd dated it. It was the anniversary of Del's death…the anniversary of her meeting Phoenix. Three years to the day.

I no longer miss the idea of you, the entry said. *I am loved. I have all I need. I'm going to school now, too, and I like it. I have friends.*

There were a few blank spaces, as if she'd had to think about what she would say next. Sev's eyes flicked down to the last sentence, her mouth going dry.

I'm sorry you died.

She swallowed, her throat clicking. She flipped to the next blank page and set her pen to paper, starting to write. The scratch of pen on paper comforted her. She wrote in steady lines, pouring memory and meaning onto the page. The words came rushing forth; writing came as easily as breathing, just as it always had.

When Soren returned, dressed for bed with damp hair curling at his temples, he eased down beside her and handed her the blanket off the back of the couch.

"What are you working on?" he asked, glancing at the journal in her lap, but careful not to invade her privacy.

She spread the blanket over them. "An old story," she murmured. She wrote a little more, then let the journal close, capping her pen and setting the book aside. Sev realized it wasn't an old story at all; she still had so much more ahead of her.

His smile was soft, touched by the firelight. "Read it to me?"

She shook her head, clutching her journal to her chest. "Don't know how it ends yet," she said with a smirk. "You'll have to wait."

He chuckled. "Fair enough. Want to call your dad?"

Sev nodded, pressing her hand gently over his. His skin was warm from the shower. "Yeah. I think I'm ready," she said. "It's quiet without them."

Soren tilted his head. "Bad quiet?"

She shook her head, brushing her thumb across the back of his hand. "No," she said. "It's good."

And it was.

There was the held breath of an unknown journey ahead of her, the comfort of companionship beside her. Sev could hardly wait to see what came next.

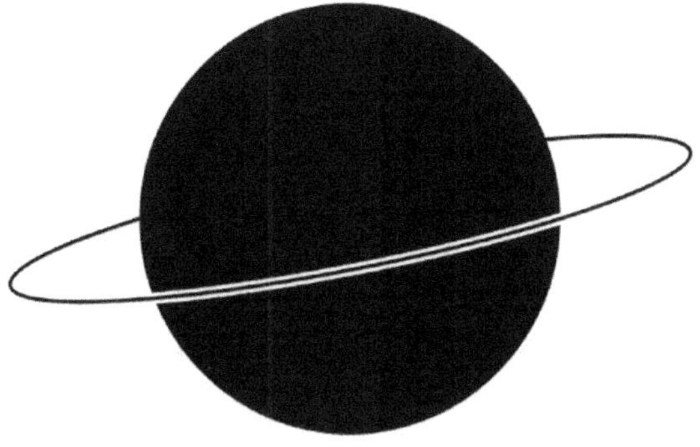

213

About the Author

Jessahme Wren is an award-winning science fiction author who writes character-driven stories about resilience, hope, and found family. Her Terra series blends emotional depth with immersive worldbuilding, exploring what it means to heal, to belong, and to fight for the people we love.

A long-time educator, Jessahme brings compassion and humanity to every story she creates. When she isn't writing, she enjoys reading, traveling, spending time with family, and relaxing with her two pets. She is currently working on future books in the Terra series.

Keep up to date on news and all my books here:

Thank you for purchasing this book.
If you enjoyed your read, please provide feedback in the
form of a review.